CRAZY LIFE OF AN ADORABLE FAT GIRL

BERNICE BLOOM

COPYRIGHT

CRAZY LIFE OF AN ADORABLE FAT GIRL

Hello, Welcome to book three which continues the adventures of the delicious, larger-than-life Mary Brown. In this book, Mary returns to fat club and reunites with the cast of funny characters who graced book one. But this time there is a new fat club member... a glamorous blonde who Mary takes against.

Mary is also facing troubles in her relationship with Ted, and she reveals why she has been suffering from an eating disorder for most of her life. What incident caused are all these problems?

I really hope you enjoy reading about our delightful, overweight heroine.

Lots of love, Bernice xx

1. NO KNICKERS AND A RED FACE

*T*he door to the beauty salon made a welcoming sound as I opened it. A kind of a tinkling sound, as if I were entering a wonderful world of fairy magic.

Going to the beauticians is one of my favourite things in the whole world. All the gorgeous smells and the wildly over-made-up women in their nurse-like outfits drifting around talking in warm and calming voices; I think it's that combination of a woman who really loves her makeup (I mean *really* loves makeup – some of them wear so much of the stuff that their foundation enters the room five minutes before the rest of them), and a pseudo- scientific approach to the job, that makes them so appealing.

You know what I mean about the science – those uniforms they wear and all the talk of alpha hydroxides, illuminating particles and oxygen carrying molecules – I'm convinced every time that my life will be transformed by these women and their alluring potions and endless promises.

"This will make you look 10 years younger," a beautician with a sleepy smile will say.

"I will make your pores invisible and your wrinkles vanish."

"I will make you grow six inches taller and you'll become President of the United States of America."

OK, maybe not the last two, but you know what I mean. Who doesn't want to be in a world in which everyone is telling you they will make you look better? It's like the most perfect world ever.

The science is great, and very compelling – the beautician peers at your skin under a light so bright that it could light up the sky, staring at your skin with an intensity and determination normally reserved for nuclear fusion and brain surgery. It is as if the beauty technician is solving all the problems of the universe: you expect her to make a pronouncement about string theory or black holes, but she doesn't do that, she declares that you need a deluxe, rabbit ear facial or some other such tosh and your skin will be perfect. And you believe her. Well – I do. She could suggest absolutely anything to me at that stage and I'd be fine with it.

"We will spray essence of sea breeze onto your skin along with crushed crab heads." Fine.

"We'll cover your face in horse manure and dance around you, waving tea towels." Great.

"We'll put salt in your eyes and vinegar in your ears and sing the national anthem." Perfect.

Christ. It's so ridiculous.

And I'm absolutely sure every time that they cover my face in something like mashed up beetles' legs, sea moss and elephant semen that I'll emerge looking like Cameron Diaz. Because that's the thing about going to the beauticians – it's all about the hope. Hope of a prettier face, better skin, a tighter jaw line. It's all about the triumph of optimism over common sense.

I always think that this might be the one time that I leave after the treatments looking really different, really special. Alas, dear readers, I have to report that – to date – no treatment I've had has ever made the blindest bit of difference to the way I look. But I keep going. I keep turning up at the door with the tinkling sounds in the hope that it will work *this* time.

. . .

So, I went to the beauticians for a facial. They showed me through to a small 'consulting' room. I wasn't really sure whether I should get undressed and lie down on the bed, or wait for the beautician.

No one told me to get undressed, but clearly I knew I had to remove my top and I didn't want to look like a complete beauty amateur by waiting to be told everything, but – equally – I didn't want to be presumptuous. On balance I'd rather wait to be told, so I sat down and looked at the rows and rows of lotions, creams and sprays on the side, and enjoyed the strong smell of lavender sitting heavily in the air. The creams and lotions had alluring names – all of them promising to have a transformational effect upon the user. Whether you wanted to look younger, tighter, plumper or glossier, you could do so by simply picking up the relevant bottle and smearing the contents on your face.

I reached over and took one of the bottles. It said 'youth serum'. I couldn't resist it. I glanced at the door, then twisted the cap and attempted to put a couple drops of the serum into my hand. But I twisted the cap too much and tonnes of the bloody gloopy stuff came out. The liquid smelled like almonds but had the consistency of semen, which unnerved me a little. I rubbed the semen serum into my face. I'd just covered the right side of my face when the door opened and the beautician walked in. I quickly rubbed my hand against the towel on the bed next to me so she didn't know I'd been pinching her almond semen.

"Hello," she said, extending a very tiny, perfectly manicured hand. I reached out to shake it and watched in dismay at how much bigger my hand was than hers. Mine looked like a man's hand. A fat man's hand. Who on earth wants a fat man's hand? I bet even a fat man doesn't want a fat man's hand.

While we shook hands and exchanged polite greetings, I could feel the right side of my face tingling. It wasn't unpleasant – just a gentle feeling of warmth spreading through it. It felt nice. It felt like the serum was working – yay!

But no.

No.

What a disaster. I only had the serum on one side of my face. I became suddenly paranoid that one side of my face would look years younger than the other. I pictured half of me looking like Taylor Swift and the other half Theresa May. Not a good look.

The beautician was very exotic. If she were a smell she'd be cherry blossom and magnolia or lemon grass and pear (see how obsessed I was becoming with the smells? See how this place has got to me?). She sat down and asked me what my concerns were about my skin. Really, I didn't know how much time she'd got, but I did have a lot of concerns. I began to reel them off…the redness around my nose, the puffiness around my eyes, the spots on my chin, the oily patch down the centre of my face. And the open pores. My God! My pores were so open I could store things in them. And wrinkles – don't forget the wrinkles!

"You're being very hard on yourself," she said in a foreign accent so strong that I could barely understand her. She sounded like she was from South Africa. "You have lovely skin and it will look even lovelier after the facial."

There we go…the promises, the hope, the optimism…

She had the most beautiful, caramel-coloured skin and gorgeous shiny black hair. There was more fat in my thumb than she had in her entire body.

"I'm going to go out of the room to let you get yourself sorted. Could you remove your knickers and lie back on the bed. Get yourself comfortable and I'll be back in a tick."

The lady moved to leave the room.

"Sorry, could you repeat that?" I said. She couldn't really want me to remove my knickers, could she?

"Just lie back on the bed," she said in her clipped accent. "Make yourself comfortable, and remember to remove your knickers. I'll be back in just a minute."

I knew I should run after her really, and ask her why on earth I had to remove my most intimate piece of clothing when I was having a facial. But I didn't, of course. In the same way that I don't scream "it's too bloody hot" if I'm at the hairdressers and they wash my hair in boiling water.

"Is the temperature OK?" the girl will ask, and even though my scalp is melting under her fingers, I say "yes, it's fine," knowing I'll have to go straight to A&E for a scalp transplant afterwards.

So, I took my knickers off and settled down on the bed with a small towel covering my embarrassment.

A few minutes later the lady came back in, smiled at me and took the towel off me.

"Whaaaaa…" she said, staring at me. "Why the hell did you remove your knickers?"

"You told me to," I insisted.

She backed away, towards the door, and looked at me as if I was completely mad.

"I said remove your necklace. Your necklace. Not your knickers."

"Ohhhh…"

I struggled back into my underwear and lay back on the bed. "Sorry," I muttered, as the smell of ylang-ylang and sandalwood filled the room. "I thought you said knickers. I wouldn't have taken them off otherwise. I'm not the sort of person who…"

"Sssshhh… just relax," she said as she massaged some sort of concoction that smelled like the earth into my face. "Relax and think about how beautiful you are going to look."

"OK." I sensed myself drifting away. "OK, I'll relax."

The facial was lovely. I almost fell asleep as she covered my face in a thick, heavy paste and said, to my delight, "I'm going to give you a massage while the face masque is doing its magic. She started to apply oil to her hands which she then began to massage into my legs and I began to really relax, but then I couldn't help but think about her tiny, delicate hands and how horrible it must be for her to have to massage my enormous, fat thighs. I wondered whether she was repulsed. She was so tiny, so small and delicate, I bet she'd never seen thighs as enormous as mine. As she massaged away I experienced an overwhelming urge to explain (lie) to her about why I was so fat.

Of course, the reason I was overweight was because I ate too much, but that's not much of a story is it? So I told her all about my baby that had just been born. In fact, I told her I'd just had twins.

"How lovely," she said. "I'm so envious. I'd love to have a baby one day. Twins would be amazing. I'd love that more than anything in the world. How long ago did you have them?"

"Yesterday," I replied. (I know, I know, stupid answer, but I was under pressure and not thinking straight…what, with all the lavender and massaging and everything.)

"YESTERDAY?"

"Yep."

"My God. Really? That's amazing. I'll be really gentle with the massage," she said. "You probably shouldn't be here so soon afterwards."

"I'm fine. Honestly," I said, wishing I'd never embarked on this line of chatter. I really wanted her to carry on massaging me firmly. I love firm massages.

"Where are the twins now?"

"Sorry?"

"The twins…I wondered where they were."

"My friend has them outside."

"So sweet," said the beautiful therapist and I nodded in agreement in the darkness of the room. My imaginary babies were, indeed, very sweet.

"What are their names?"

"Pardon."

"I just wondered what their names were?" she asked.

Bugger.

"William and Kate," I said, without thinking.

"Oh. Nice. Very patriotic," she replied.

"Yes."

"OK, that's the end of the treatment. Has everything been OK for you?"

"Lovely," I mumbled. My skin was tingling like crazy, my shoulders were relaxed and I had two amazing imaginary babies named after a future King and Queen of England.

"I'm just going to turn the light up a little bit."

She padded gently towards the door. "Don't get up quickly, take it easy, especially since you had your babies yesterday."

"Yeah, don't worry too much about the whole baby thing," I said. "Really, it was quite simple, no aggro."

"Holy fuck."

"What's the matter?" I asked as she stared at me, her face in her hands, her eyes wide as saucers.

"It's your face. Something weird has happened to your face – it's absolutely scarlet."

2. THE TROUBLE WITH TED

*I*t would have been a lie to say that my skin looked better after the facial; it would have been more accurate to describe me as looking like I'd been peeled and pickled. Yep, we'd need a whole new word for red. The beautician said that the 'blush' (BLUSH? I looked like I'd been boiled!) would go down within a few hours and I should make sure I didn't put any makeup on for 24 hours to get the full benefits of the treatment. So I was heading off to my friend Charlie's house looking like someone had rubbed a cheese grater against my face then sprinkled vinegar on top. Great! And I'd paid for it. And couldn't put any makeup on it to make it less angry-looking. Marvellous.

Charlie's my best, and oldest friend. She's known me forever and we used to do absolutely everything together when we were younger. She opened the door and gave me a huge hug, then she released me and glanced at my face before jumping back in horror. Her hands flew to her mouth.

"Good God, you look as if you've been attacked by wolves!" she said.

"No, no, I'm fine."

"Car crash?"

"No, honestly, I'm fine."

"Late onset meningitis?"

"No really, I just went for a facial today and I seem to have reacted to some of the products."

"Yeah, I'll say. *Reacted* is a bit of an understatement. Why's it so much worse on the right side of your face?"

"No idea."

"OK. And you're absolutely sure you don't need a doctor."

"Positive," I said. "The beautician wasn't at all alarmed and neither should I be."

This was a lie – the beautician was very alarmed; she screamed when she saw the colour I'd gone, and called for urgent assistance. The owner of the beauty salon came running down the corridor as fast as her silk Chinese slippers would allow her and threw cold water on my face. The red didn't fade. In fact it looked worse when wet. The two women looked at one another – completely out of options. "I think you need to go home and relax and it should fade," said one of them.

"Yes," said the other enthusiastically, as if her colleague had just solved the mysteries of the universe. "Sandra's right; it should fade. Just go and relax."

Despite their apparent conviction that going home (i.e. getting out of their salon before anyone saw me) was the best thing to do, they kept glancing one another in a way which screamed *'what the fuck do we do now?'*

"OK, well I guess the beauticians know what they're talking about," said Charlie. "Come on, come in." She swept her arm into the house for me to follow her inside, still staring at my face in a kind of squinty fashion as if she couldn't quite believe what she was seeing.

"How are you? I mean – besides the raw tomato face thing."

"I'm fine, really. I'm a lot better than I look."

"Christ, yes, I imagine you are. How is Ted?"

I was dreading this question. The truth was that Ted was great. He was kind and decent and honest and he loved me. But for some reason... I didn't know how...we were sort of drifting apart, and I found myself struggling to understand why. I didn't feel as madly in love with him as I used to be, and he was starting to annoy me quite a lot.

"Everything OK?" she asked. "I mean – Ted-wise?"

Charlie had heard everything she needed to know in my silence.

"Everything's not OK, is it?" she said. "Do you want to talk?"

"Everything's sort of fine," I replied. "I mean it's not *not fine* or anything."

"Sort of fine? Not *not fine?*"

"Sort of," I repeated.

"Glass of wine?"

"A large one would be great, thanks."

I followed her into the kitchen, jumping as I saw my bright red face in the hall mirror. I looked as if I was in a permanent state of extreme anger.

Charlie handed me a drink and we clinked glasses affectionately.

"So, things aren't going well with Ted?" she said.

"I don't know, Charlie. I'm not being evasive or anything, I just don't know. It's not that things aren't going well, it's just that I'm not really feeling it… Do you know what I mean? I don't know…"

"Have you spoken to Ted about this?" she asked. "Last time we had any sort of conversation about him you were ludicrously happy and heading off to stalk him in Amsterdam while wearing a pink onesie and clutching a kite. What happened to change your mind?"

"That was ages ago. Things have changed a bit recently. I haven't spoken to him because I don't know what I'd say to him. I mean – it's not like I don't love him. And, yes, I know, I was obsessed with him… could think of nothing else. And he has done nothing wrong, and nothing has changed but I've sort of done this mental thing where I've switched off and gone off him. I don't know…it's nuts. Perhaps I'll just get over it."

I should mention, for anyone who hasn't read my previous books, that Ted and I have been seeing each other for a few months. We started going out together at the end of this Fat Club course that we both attended. Did I tell you I'm really fat? No? Well, I am, and so is he. We both lost some weight on the Fat Club course, but we both have loads to go. I need to shift a minimum of six more stone before I am anywhere near fighting weight. He's bigger – he reckons he is nine stone off his ideal weight. I know what you're thinking – that's a lot, that's like two extra people we're carrying around with us. And you're right – but we are trying to lose the weight.

Since meeting on the Fat Club course we have carried on seeing one another all summer. We've had an amazing time, spending most nights of the week together and all weekend. Infact we rarely went out. We seemed to spend all our time inside cuddling up together, watching TV or watching films. I think that if it weren't for Fat Club we'd have spent most of our time eating takeaways and drinking wine, because – let's be honest – that's a bloody marvellous way to pass the time, but we were good, and we cooked instead of getting takeaways. I even persuaded Ted to try salads, against his better judgement (believing green food was the stuff of the devil). I gave him an apple but when he bit into it the made the most extraordinary face – full of pain and anguish. "There's no chocolate in mine," he said, in the manner of a seven-year-old who's woken up on Christmas morning to no presents.

We had fun though – we had BBQs in the summer, sometimes inviting friends round, but usually with just the two if us. In fact – yes – it was just the two of us. Now I come to think of it we only talked of inviting other people round, but never actually got round to it, preferring to spend time alone, together. It was lovely – lying in the garden when it was warm, or in front of the TV later in the summer when things got colder. To be fair, we spent most of our time lying around. I wonder whether that was why the spark went. It's early November now and we were still lying around.

I suppose, when you think about it, it's not hard to see why things have gone a bit askew with me and Ted, is it? Fundamentally, it's quite boring to do the same thing every day. The other thing is I realise that I stopped making an effort. In the early days of the relationship I only had to think he might be coming round and I'd be thrown into a wild frenzy of cleaning and organising the house, then shaving, moisturising, fake tanning and making myself up. It was exhausting. But fun. And seeing Ted's face when I opened the door always made it worthwhile. I guess somewhere along the line I stopped trying. I stopped dressing up for Ted. After all, what was the point? We were just lying on the sofa. I'd have a quick shower and brush my hair, but I was always in leggings and big, baggy t-shirts, not the lovely little 50s style dresses that I'd worn all the time when we first met and that Ted had loved so much.

I had to face the truth, as the summer had slipped into autumn, I'd stopped trying, and so had Ted. To be fair, this wasn't a one-way abandonment of the relationship. I think we were equally to blame. Ted would come round and let himself in, and I'd be sitting on the sofa, watching TV, or in the kitchen sorting things out. I'd make a cup of tea or (more likely) pour us a glass of wine and we'd both sit down on the sofa and that was our life. Gosh, when you look at it in black-and-white like that it's amazing we lasted so long.

The truth is that Ted and I had drifted into this space of existing together without really living or loving one another. It was a space that was – well – a bit empty.

"It sounds like you need to talk to him," said Charlie. "Tell him you still love him but that you're concerned...you're not sure that things are as good as they were."

"But that'll just worry him. You know what he's like...he'll be in a real panic. What would I say? 'You are as lovely as ever, as considerate, kind and loving as you've ever been, but I just don't know whether we are really meant to be together, I no longer feel one bit excited when I think of you.'"

"No, maybe don't say that to him...that would be a bit harsh...but tell him that the two of you need to talk."

"Talk? All we do is bloody talk."

Charlie looked at me over the rim of her wine glass. It was quite a stern look that said 'don't fuck this up; Ted's a good guy.' And she was right. Ted was the all-time, ultimate good guy.

"Perhaps it's a passing thing." As I spoke I recalled the million butterflies I used to feel every time I saw him. I wished it was still like that. I wished that every time the phone rang I prayed it was him, but I didn't. And I didn't know whether that was because we were settling into a relationship in a really normal, healthy way, or whether this was the end of the infatuation period and the end of Ted and Mary. How does anyone know?

"I guess it's just become predictable and unexciting," I said. "That's not only his fault...it's my fault as well." As I spoke, my phone vibrated on the table and I knew straight away that it was Ted.

"You see – this is the problem – there's no mystery or excitement. I always know it's him," I said, turning over the phone to show Charlie what I meant, but instead of Ted's name on the screen, it was Dave's. More specifically it said *"Dishy Dave – hottie from downstairs."*

"Oh," said Charlie. "The hottie downstairs appears to be calling."

If I hadn't already been the colour of a hot chilli, I would have gone red. Why was Dave calling? Dishy Dave lived below me and I'll confess that I have had a few entanglements with him over the years. They'd never ended well for me because he was really, really gorgeous and had lots of other options, but if he got desperate, he called me. I guess he thought that a fat female was better than no female. I'd had a few lively encounters with him as a result of this mindset, and I was very grateful every time (I have been known to thank him profusely during the course of the encounters, but let's not dwell on that now).

"So, are the problems with Ted anything to do with this Downstairs Dave?" asked Charlie.

"No," I said, in all honesty. "Nothing to do with Double D." I hadn't been anywhere near the delicious man in the flat below me since I'd started seeing Ted. I hadn't wanted to.

I didn't know why Dave was ringing me, but it had to be something to do with him borrowing something, needing something or wanting me to keep an eye out for the latest glamorous blonde in his life. It wouldn't be to fix up an illicit meeting with me, sadly.

The times he'd called in the past had been notable for their lack of any actual interest in me.

There was one occasion when he called and said: "Tesco's are bringing my shopping, are you in to collect it?"

The honest answer was: "No, I'm not in."

Is that what I said to him?

Of course not. I wanted to be useful. I wanted to be the one to whom he turned when he needed anything. All in the vain hope that he'd realise one day, like the characters in every decent romantic comedy ever made, that the woman of his dreams was right beneath his nose all the time.

So, I said: "Sure, no problem. I'm here. I can help." Even though I wasn't, not by a long chalk, I was bloody miles away at Mum and Dad's house and had to leave mid-sentence with barely an explanation and break the land speed record to get home in time for the Tesco man.

"I'll call you later to explain," I'd shouted to Dad over my shoulder as I waddled at speed through the streets like a woman possessed. I'd flown towards the shared gate that led to mine and Dave's flats just as the Tesco lorry was driving off.

"Stop," I screeched, and it ground to a halt, reversing back into a parking space and beginning to unload bags of shopping. I signed for it all, found Dave's spare key under the bucket in the plants, and let myself into his filthy flat.

I put the shopping away (to be fair – it was mainly beer), then had a huge tidy up and sat down to wait for Dave's return. In my head he'd be so delighted that I'd stepped into the breach and not only brought in his shopping and put it away, but also tidied everything up, that he would instantly fall in love with me and ask me to marry him.

In the end, he didn't get home until 2am and had a glamorous blonde on his arm. I was a good 10 stone heavier than her (I really mean that – the woman can't have been more than eight stone for God's sake).

"What are you doing here?" asked Dave, quite angry, and not mentioning the vast amount of tidying up I'd done.

I slinked back to my flat and cried and ate a load of crisps.

Things like that happened a lot with me and Dave.

In fact, you could say that the only things that ever happened between me and Dave were like that.

So, on this occasion, I didn't take the call, and I switched my phone off.

"Right," I said to Charlie. "Let's talk about you; tell me what you've been up to."

"Well, it's funny you should ask," she said. "Did I tell you about Sam? The guy I met on Tinder."

"No." I poured more wine into my glass and went to put the bottle down when the glass was half-full.

"I strongly think that this is a large glass of wine sort of story," said Charlie, tipping so much wine into my glass that it was full to the brim and I could barely lift it. She filled her own glass.

"Well, he seemed nice...seemed normal," she said. "The picture on the site was good – he seemed to have hair and teeth and no facial tattoos...always a good start."

She told me how they'd met at the train station and he had a small bunch of flowers for her.

"A really nice touch," we agreed.

They went for a drink first and he mentioned his wife who died in a car crash 10 years earlier.

"Christ, how awful," I said. "How did she die?"

"She died when a car veered onto the pavement and hit her. She was taking their son to nursery at the time."

"Bloody hell, mate. That's awful."

"Yep. It's unbelievably awful. I felt so sorry for him. The trouble was, the whole date was all about his tragic story of lost-love. He didn't ask me anything about me. He didn't seem interested in who I was, or what I wanted, he was just glad to have someone to talk to about his late wife. Does that sound really harsh or selfish? It probably is, isn't it?"

"No, I know what you mean. It's a very sad story, but you still have to find a way to have a relationship. He has to ask something about your life, and not use you as free therapy. Tell me what happened afterwards. Did he take you home? Anything exciting happen?"

"We went for dinner, which was really nice – just in a pub in

Esher. The food was amazing…really good. Then I invited him back to mine for coffee."

"Oooooo. Now it's starting to sound exciting." I bent over in an ungainly fashion to sip from the top of my wine glass because I couldn't pick the bloody thing up – there was too much wine in it.

"He said 'yes' he'd love to come in for coffee and would drive me home. I commented that I'd noticed he wasn't drinking anything and he said 'I haven't drunk a drop of alcohol since the moment that car hit my wife' and that was it – he was off again with all the detail…all the bloody, gory detail about her blood-stained sweater and going limp in his arms. It kind of killed the mood, to be honest. I didn't feel very sexy when he was moodily moaning about blood on the street.

"Then, just as I thought things couldn't get any worse, we get into the car, he turns the key and we head off in slightly the wrong direction. 'I think we're better off turning right here,' I say to him, pointing to the next junction.

"'No, let's go this way,' he insisted. 'I want to show you where the car hit her.'"

"Fuck," I said, downing the rest of my wine in one huge mouthful and struggling to swallow it without choking and spluttering.

"That's what I said. I asked him not to take me to where she bloody died, but he insisted. Honestly, Mary, hang on to Ted, he's a good guy and there are lots of nutters out there."

"Yes," I replied, rendered almost speechless by her tale. "Yes, you're probably right."

I got home that evening and forgot that my phone had been off. It's a weird thing when you're used to having it on all the time. So, I switched it on and waited patiently for all the beeps and rings to indicate that Ted had rung about 10 times, and left eight messages.

Silence.

I checked through the message folder: nothing.

I rang the answer phone: nothing.

Oh.

Ted hadn't phoned.

I wasn't expecting that.

3. HAS HIS PHONE BROKEN OR SOMETHING?

*N*o call from Ted in the morning. Nothing at all.

I didn't care, to be honest. The relationship was dying, so I guessed it was best that he had lost interest. But I wondered why he'd lost interest. I checked the phone again. No missed call. Perhaps my phone was broken? I rang myself from my landline and the mobile began singing in front of me. It was working OK. I texted myself. Yep – the text came bouncing through.

Bugger.

Whatever. I didn't care.

Except...I kind of, sort of, did care...just a little bit. This was weird. I did like him, and I wanted him to like me. I didn't want him pulling away...that wasn't in the plan at all.

I suppose the good news in it all was that I'd be seeing Ted every Tuesday night from now on at Fat Club, because it re-started that evening. Yay! The second course.

I was quite excited that it was starting up again. I knew it didn't say much for my social life that I was really thrilled to be spending an evening talking about calories and self-control, but I'd made loads of great friends on the first course (including Ted) and it would be nice to catch up with everyone again. Also I was really hoping I could get back into the weight losing groove, and shed a couple more stone.

So, when evening descended on Cobham I was on the bus and heading to the crumbling community centre that passed as home for Fat Club. I got a little shiver of familiarity as I approached. I remembered walking in on the first day and thinking that this really wasn't for me, but then – by the end of the course – I was totally sold on it. Suddenly my mind was flooded with memories of meeting Ted there. He was so loveable, kind and gorgeous. Fat, of course, or why else would he have been there? And not conventionally good-looking at all – kind of half-shy, half wildly over-confident. Sometimes he would smile at me and nudge me quietly when no one was looking and I'd feel a shiver of excitement run through me. God, it's always so amazing at the beginning of a relationship, isn't it? Pity so many of them turn to shit after a few months.

As well as seeing Ted at Fat Club, I'd also see the other friends I'd made, because they were all coming back for this second course. The first course had all been about losing weight – this one was about losing *more* weight. Guess what the next course was called? 'Losing *even* more weight.' Not sure what would happen after that: 'Losing so much weight it's unbelievable', 'Coping with being too thin'? I don't know. All I did know was that the first course worked like a dream – I felt happier, more confident and – crucially! – thinner after it, so I was going in again.

I walked inside, and saw I was the third person to arrive. Liz, the course leader, was in the room, standing at the front in an apple green jumper and a purple skirt, sorting out her notes, while Janice chatted away to her.

"And then he killed his wife and ran off with the butcher's son!" she was saying. "Can you believe that?"

"Blimey," I said. "You don't half socialise with some colourful characters."

"No, not my social life. This is the plot of the book that Liz told me to read."

"That's a relief." I waddled over to Janice and gave her a kiss on the cheek. "I was worried about you for a minute then."

"Hi, Liz, are you OK?" I kissed her on the cheek as well. "What have you got planned for us then? Anything weird or complicated?"

"Nothing weird," said Liz. "We'll just be doing more of what we did on the first course, but probing; trying to find out why people are eating too much, why it's become a crutch. We will be leaning on each other for moral support."

"OK – sounds good," I said. "I never thought I'd say this but I've missed the regular group meetings, it'll be really nice to get into them again."

"That's good to hear," said Liz. "Most people come back for the second course after they've been successful on the first one, and they always say it's because they find it such a supportive environment, and they miss it when the first course stops."

"Yep, that's me." I watched Liz as she continued to remove things from her large bag. She pulled out a set of weighing scales.

"What the hell?" I said.

"You're not going to weigh us?" added Janice.

"That's the spirit," said Liz, the sarcasm dripping off every word. "Be enthusiastic and encouraging."

"But – they are weighing scales," I pointed out. "Weighing scales! I'd be less terrified if you had pulled out a gun."

"You're not going to weigh us?" repeated Janice.

"No, of course not."

"Then why would you have weighing scales?"

Honestly, bringing out weighing scales at a Fat Club is like bringing out a bomb or something. I noticed that Janice had physically recoiled from the sight of it.

"Can you put it away," she said. "You're making me feel queasy."

"Don't be silly now, ladies," said Liz, shaking her head, pushing her hand into her bag and pulling out a tape measure.

"Whooooah. And you can put that back from where you got it as well," said Janice.

"I'm not going to use them to measure you with, if that's what you're worried about."

"That's what I'm very worried about," said Janice. "Why would you have them if you weren't going to use them on us?"

"Yes," I added in a slightly trembling voice, unable to take my eyes off the scales.

"Oh, for goodness' sake." Liz put them back in her bag. "You two are ridiculous. You've both done so well and lost so much weight. Isn't it time to be proud of how much you weigh?"

"Proud?" I said. "I'm six bloody stone overweight, proud is certainly not how I'm feeling."

It's one thing discussing our difficulties with food, and trying to learn to readjust and alter our mindsets, but it's quite another thing to be humiliated publicly. If people knew how much I weighed they'd be astonished I was able to walk properly without my legs breaking beneath me.

"Hi," I said as Veronica walked into the room and saw us all staring at Liz as she stuffed the scales and tape measure into her bag.

"Oooo…what are they for? I'm not being weighed, not for anyone."

"Not another one," said Liz. "They're not for weighing."

"What on earth are they for then?" asked Veronica.

Liz continued to put the scales into her bag, and to remove notes, books and what looked like a skipping rope.

"I'm not skipping either – you can forget about that. With boobs this size I'd knock myself out."

"Will you lot stop worrying. Nothing terrible is going to happen. You're not going to have to do anything. These are for my next class – not for you. I was just checking that I have everything I need. So you can all just relax."

"I can't relax with that skipping rope on the table…it's terrifying. I feel like I'm back in school and am not invited to join in the skipping games."

"Bloody hell, ladies – you're hard work tonight." Liz put the skipping rope back into the bag with the scales and tape measure. She looked up. "Happy now?"

"Much happier," said Veronica with a smile. I'd forgotten how attractive Veronica is. She was a former model with the loveliest face ever – like a doll's. She had porcelain skin…kind of like Sophie Dahl used to look before she lost all that weight and let us all down. Veronica's big, but she was in proportion and very curvy…I mean *very*. Huge big breasts that probably had their own postcode and a big squishy bottom that I'm sure men adored.

She was a real sweetie but I confess that I didn't like her at first. She was quite stand-offish and it seemed like she wanted to tell everyone that she used to be a model all the time, like we were supposed to treat her differently or something. Perhaps I was jealous? I don't know, but I didn't really want to be around her, then – after the end of the first course she was very sweet to me, and we ended up going shopping together and became friends. And we went on a road trip to Amsterdam that was a bit of a disaster. Now I really like her.

She told me about how she'd always wanted to be a model and was devastated when it ended. She felt like a complete failure and felt like she wasn't qualified to do anything else. I realised she kept saying that she used to be a model because she felt that was all she had going for her. Far from showing off, she was desperately insecure and trying to hide the insecurity. I like her a lot and I was sure she would always be a friend.

"You OK, gorgeous?" she said.

"I'm fine, thanks."

She sat next to me so I had Janice one side and Veronica the other. For a fleeting moment I thought to myself that I should ask her to move so Ted could sit next to me. But then I remembered that Ted hadn't called or texted or made any effort to get in touch with me for two days. TWO DAYS! He was dead to me. I was glad to be in the middle of a Janice and Veronica sandwich.

"Where's Ted?" asked Veronica, as if she could read my mind.

"He's not here yet." I tried to sound as neutral and unbothered as possible. "I'm sure he'll be here soon."

"Hello," came a voice from the doorway – it was Phil and his wife. They were both elderly, and they were the only people I didn't really get to know on the last course. They sat together, quietly and didn't chat to us or join in any of our post-session drinks, and they were quiet during the sessions themselves. All I knew about them was that they were both called Phil: Philippa and Philip, known as the Phils. They said that at their work (because not only did they have the same name, they also worked in the same place) they were known as the Fat Phils. I laughed out loud when she said that, but the look on Philippa's face told me that it wasn't a laughing matter. In fact it was a major bone of contention and she absolutely hated that they were known in such derogatory terms.

I was determined to make friends with them on this course, and spend a bit of time getting to know them. They seemed like nice people and it was a shame that they weren't properly part of the group simply because they arrived in a couple and not on their own like the rest of us. I was determined to pull them into the centre of our little group. I'd be the club's social secretary.

The masculine Phil was resplendent in a large overcoat and the feminine Phil sported a sturdy-looking winter coat in a kind of boiled wool, dyed olive green. Possibly the most unflattering coat ever made. She was wearing brown tights and lace-up brown shoes exactly the same colour so that her legs blended seamlessly into her feet – like she'd got hooves. The shoes were deeply unattractive – the type of orthopaedic shoes that might be given to a child with an unfortunate birth condition that has resulted in one leg growing longer than the other.

Veronica watched as I walked over to them, with a quizzical look on her face. "I'm the social secretary," I whispered to her and Janice.

When I reached the Phils and smiled: "We never really got to know each other on the last course," I said.

"No," said Phil, in a way which made it sound as if that was entirely by design, and he was eager to avoid us getting to know one another on this one.

"I'm Mary," I said, smiling broadly.

"You have lipstick on your teeth, Mary," said Philippa. For Christ's sake, could she not just smile and shake my hand? I was trying my hardest here.

I rubbed my tongue across my front teeth.

"We should all make more of an effort to get to know each other this time," I said, and Philippa looked quite terrified. "I mean – we hardly spoke to one another on the last course…why don't you come out for a drink with us one night?"

"We don't drink," said Phil.

"Well, come and have a Coke or coffee or something?" I tried.

"I don't think so," he said. "Thanks for asking."

I turned round to return to my seat and walked straight into Janice. "I don't want to be social secretary any longer," I told her. "The job's yours."

As I sat down I was still running my tongue along the front of my teeth to make sure the lipstick had all gone. This was the problem with bright red lipstick – if it got anywhere but your lips it looked bloody awful…collars, sleeves and especially teeth.

I decided on red lips today to match my red dress. I was wearing it to show Ted what he was missing. He liked me in red. I liked me in red. So I was slightly confused as to why I'd been wearing grey leggings and t-shirts all summer. It was quite a figure-hugging dress for me and I felt ever so slightly self-conscious, but I knew this was a dress that Ted really liked, and even though I didn't care a damn about him and, frankly, didn't care whether he turned up or not that night, I wanted him to be impressed if he did.

Oh God. He was here.

I subconsciously tidied my hair as I saw him appear through the door. My stomach was in knots…probably because of the food I'd eaten earlier. I'd made a spicy chicken salad. Not the best decision in the world for someone who was rubbish when it came to eating spicy foods. Then I noticed. He was wearing the blue jumper I'd given him. Ahhhh, he looked really, really nice. God, I'd missed him. Why had I decided I didn't like him any more? I did like him…I mean – really liked him – look at him – he was just lovely.

Ted walked towards me and I didn't know what to do. We'd been ignoring each other and I didn't know why. I had butterflies in my stomach and I felt madly self-conscious. I looked down and started pretending to dig into my bag for something. When I looked up, he had gone over to talk to Liz, and was kissing her on both cheeks and asking her about the course. Fuck. Why was I behaving like such an idiot?

Ted looked good, I had to admit that. He'd taken the jumper off and you could see clearly that, in common with most of us, he'd lost a few stone since the first course and it really suited him. He had jeans on with the shirt tucked into them, and while no one could accuse him of being too thin, I could remember the days when he would only wear the baggiest of shirts, and they always hung outside his jeans. He used to walk around with a look of desperate embarrassment at his own existence. That had turned to mild confidence. He looked like a man who was comfortable in his skin. It was amazing what losing weight could do for a person.

It was great to see everyone back in the room where we'd first met; there was a real familiarity, warmth and happiness in being with these people with whom I'd been through so much.

We'd all lost weight since the last course, but more importantly than that, we'd all realised why we were eating so much. We'd all listened to the lectures and heard each other's stories. We understood that we had convinced ourselves, somewhere deep down, that eating was going to make us feel better, feel loved, or feel so full that we wouldn't worry any more about the problems that seemed to haunt us like ghosts in the night.

Through my eating I was literally trying to smother all the problems I had. The great irony for me was the discovery that the 'problems' I had were largely related to my self-esteem, and that self-esteem hinged on what I looked like. So – for heaven's sake – every time I ate to hide my problems, I was making my problems worse because I felt more unattractive to myself as I got bigger, which ate away at my diminishing self-esteem.

Coming onto the first course helped me recognise that, and put a stop to it. I did some sort of psychological switch whereby I knew I wasn't eating because I was hungry – I was eating to make myself feel good, and I stopped it. I did other things that made me feel good – things like walking and swimming, and the weight started to come off. The more it came off, the happier I felt, and the less inclined I was to eat

I hadn't been perfect, and I had strayed from the straight and narrow at times, which was why I'd been eager for the class to start up again, but I'd been pretty good, all in all. Sure, I could eat a packet of biscuits in one sitting, and if you saw me wolf down a bag of chips you'd think that my psychological problems were as bad as ever, but they're weren't. I'd eat and eat and eat and then I'd have a moment of lucidity when I realised what I was doing and I'd stop. I'd never had those feelings of lucidity before. To be honest, I never stopped until I started crying or started feeling sick. Since the first course I could still eat loads and loads but then I'd think 'what the hell are you doing, woman?' and I'd stop. And I didn't do it again the next day and the day after.

4. THE NEW GIRL AT FAT CLUB

"Just waiting for one more person," said Liz, with a gentle shrug of her shoulders and a warm smile. Liz had been such a support to me since the last course ended: phoning up to keep me on track, and making sure she checked in with me from time to time, just to make sure I was OK.

"No, we're all here," I said, looking around the room and smiling at everyone except Ted. I still couldn't look at him. He made me feel all nervous and jittery and I was terrified about the fact that he didn't call me or anything.

Why didn't he call me? He was supposed to like me. People who like you, call you.

He half-smiled at me, then sucked the smile in as I looked away, and I wished immediately that I hadn't looked away. Why the hell did I look away? And why the hell didn't he just come over and say hello, or talk to me, or behave like any half-normal human being would?

"Ah, but we're not all here," said Liz. "Because we have a newcomer who will be turning up for the session tonight..."

Everyone in the room looked at Liz. This was most unwelcome news. We'd become such a tight-knit group, sharing details of our issues with food and stories about failed weight loss and bonding over

26

our shared problems and fears. We trusted each other and felt comfortable with each other. We'd delved deep into our psyches and shared information with the group that was personal, sad and touching. There had been tears, smiles and anguish, as we'd talked about the deaths of those close to us and how they sent us spiralling into anguish and overeating. I felt I knew more about some of the people in that room and what they'd been through than I knew about members of my own family. How could someone new be joining us?

The door at the back of the hall opened and in walked a large woman (of course...she'd hardly be here if she was Kylie Minogue size). She was dressed beautifully, in a pair of cut-off jeans and an off-the-shoulder red and white polka dot top. She looked like she ought to be in St Tropez or something with her incredible suntan and lashings of red lipstick. I looked down at my outfit and suddenly I felt dowdy. Her red was brighter and her lips were like glistening cherries. I was not the brightest, most eye-catching person in the room any more and it disturbed me more than it should.

"I'm Michella," she said with a massive smile that stretched right across her face.

I hated that she was so pretty, but most of all I hated that she seemed so nice with it.

"Come and sit here," said Ted with a smile, indicating the seat next to him.

What?

Fuck. No.

She ran her hand through her blonde hair. It was a shade or two lighter than mine which made me really cross. I wanted to be the brightest blonde in the room. I loved having blonde hair. I'd always loved it.

I remembered being at school, and sitting on the benches at the back as a fifth former, slightly elevated from the rest of the children and looking down onto the heads in front of me. All the heads were shades of brown. Sure there was the occasional blonde head but it was mainly brown. Any blonde head would stand out like ripe corn in a muddy field and I vowed that I would always be blonde.

I remembered when I first dyed my hair, my mum and dad were really cross, but I loved it... I thought I look like a movie star. I thought I looked like my Barbie that I'd played with as a little girl. I thought I looked like a woman should look – bright, pretty and alluring but with an edge of vulnerability. I thought I looked fantastic and I've been dyeing my hair ever since. In some ways, I was quite envious of people like Janice with her mousey hair, and the fact that she felt no compunction to hide her natural state. I was all about hiding mine. I didn't want to be natural and 'myself' on the outside. If you are a mouse inside, I think you feel drawn to becoming a peacock on the outside.

"Hello, nice to meet you," she said to me, having thoroughly ingratiated herself with my boyfriend.

"I'm Mary," I said, ignoring the way Ted was smiling at me. I was sure Ted's smile was screaming: "Look, look – a pretty girl. You have been replaced..."

And no – I wasn't being paranoid.

"Have you been on a sunbed?" she asked.

"No," I replied. Most of the redness had gone out of my skin following my disastrous beauty treatment, but clearly not all of it.

"Oh, an allergy of some kind?"

"No."

"A rash?"

"No."

For God's sake, woman. Let it go, will you.

"OK, let's get started," said Liz, rising to her feet and smiling at us. "You'll have noticed that we have a new girl in our midst..."

Yes, we've all noticed, I thought to myself. There was nothing interesting about a new girl turning up, in fact it was a positive distraction. I wanted to just get on with the session and not obsess about someone new being here. But – no – of course they couldn't do that. We all had to get to know this glamorous young creature who'd crawled into our little group. To make it all worse, Michella was invited to go straight to the front of the room and give a small talk to us.

I looked at the way she walked…it was positively sick-making. Silly cow with her wiggly hips and big bottom. No one's impressed, love. No one's impressed.

"Hello, my name is Michella," she said, running a hand through her blonde hair and pushing it back over her shoulder. She was very pretty – disturbingly so. I was sure she was exactly Ted's type. Let's be honest, she looked like a prettier, younger version of me. Bitch.

"People call me 'Mich' for short," she said, looking around the room with big blue eyes framed by long eyelashes that I was sure she kept fluttering in the direction of my boyfriend. Did she really need to do that?

"OK, where do I start? I'm really overweight, as you can see. I look horrible, and I feel horrible, and I'd go as far as to say that a lot of the time I really hate myself. I want to do something about it, but for some reason I don't seem able to sort my head out and I sabotage myself every time I try to lose weight. I thought that by being in a supportive environment like this I might be able to change the way I am, and eventually lose weight. You all seem really nice, so that's a good start!"

She looked around the room, desperate for encouragement, and I knew it was really evil, but I was silently praying that no one offered her any.

"We're all here for you," said Ted, kindly, and I felt like punching him.

"Yes," added Janice. "We look after each other in this group." I feared I might explode with anger. She was such a traitor.

"I know why and when I started putting on weight – it's not a very happy story, but I feel I ought to tell you, so you fully understand me and what I've been through."

Oh great. This was obviously going to take bloody hours.

"I had a twin sister called Emily," she said, pausing for a moment before giving a faint laugh to cover up the fact that she was getting emotional. "Phew. I knew it was going to be difficult to tell you about this.

"Anyway, Emily got ill when we were young. She had leukaemia, aged just 12, I remember it like it was yesterday; like it was this morning; like it was two minutes ago. I remember it all so clearly, in fact it's like she's still here with me now, like she'll walk in any moment and hug me and we'll carry on playing with our dolls and everything will be OK. But it won't, because the leukaemia took her away from me. We can't talk about boys any more, or moan at each other for stealing each other's clothes or dance to our favourite pop music. We can't do any of it. She died and I just couldn't cope, and looking back, I was left on my own a lot after her death because my parents were struggling too. They comforted each other, they cried together and screamed together and threw themselves into the organisation of the funeral and into setting up a charitable foundation. Me? I just ate."

Michella burst into tears, holding her sides and sobbing with all her heart. I did feel sorry for her – I'm not that callous. It must be unbelievably hard to lose a twin. I mean – to lose a sister would be beyond awful, but a twin sister...that must be so much worse.

"I'm sorry, I'm really sorry, I thought it was important to talk through this because I think that's why I eat so much – because the pain is killing me and I still try to bury it under food. Even talking to you today has made me think that now I could really do with a big cream cake!"

Everybody laughed and there were more mutterings of support, and people telling her how incredibly brave she was.

Michella then went on to describe the painful death of her sister. The two of them played together until the day before she died. She spoke about how brave her sister was, never complaining, always enthusiastic and talking about the future. "She must have known that she wouldn't be here to enjoy so many of the things we spoke about, but she continued to plan and to talk about the future, and we wrote to *Top of the Pops* and said we wanted to be in the audience, and we wrote to our favourite pop stars and asked them for autographs, and in none of the letters she sent did she mention she was ill. It was like she didn't want it to affect anything. When she died, it felt that everything was pointless. The only thing that made me happy was food. The weight piled on and I didn't care, I'd get exhausted running for the bus and it didn't bother me in the least. Now, though, it does. I lost my sister half a lifetime ago, and I need to start living again. For her. She's not here to enjoy life, so I need to enjoy it doubly as much... I need to start enjoying life for her as well as for me."

When she finished, there was a huge round of applause and a standing ovation, and she stood in the middle of it all just beaming.

The rest of us went up one by one and gave short talks about what we'd done since the last course. I kept mine brief. I just talked about my weight and my eating. Then Ted went up.

"It's been the best few months ever," he told everyone. "Because I've spent so much of it with Mary."

I looked up, stunned.

"She's changed my life. I'm a better man when I'm with her."

I could feel myself staring vacantly at Ted as he spoke. Everyone was staring at me, this was surreal. Ted came up to me afterwards and wrapped his arms around me.

"I know you've been busy so we haven't been able to see much of each other, but I absolutely adore you and I miss you," he said.

"I thought you'd gone off me," I replied. "When you didn't text me last night, I thought you didn't want to go out with me."

"I was giving you space," he said. "I thought you wanted some head space. I thought I was doing the right thing."

"Yes," I said. "You were. I'm an idiot."

"Are you coming for a drink?" he said, as Liz packed her stuff away and told us she'd see us next week.

"Yes." I smiled up at him. He put his arm round me.

"And are you?" he asked Mich.

"I'd love to," she said cheerily, taking his other arm in a way which REALLY annoyed me.

"Come on, you handsome hunk," she said to Ted, and I could feel my blood pressure rising. Why did she annoy me so much? She was so flirty, it was bloody horrible.

We got to the pub and she was no better, asking Ted to choose a drink for her and stroking his hair while he did. To his credit, he looked uncomfortable with all the attention, but he didn't push her away. He didn't tell her it was inappropriate.

Eventually I couldn't do it any longer. "Right, I'm off," I said to a bewildered-looking Ted, and I stomped out of the pub without saying goodbye to anyone else. I shuffled out into the cold night air and hid around the corner from Ted who had followed me. I didn't know why. Even I was confused at the way I was behaving. If I'd gone and spoken to Ted and told him I wanted to go home, he'd have taken me. And that would have been all my problems solved – I'd get him to myself and away from Michella. Bingo! But for some reason I couldn't bring myself to make life easy. I couldn't bring myself to run into his arms and make everything right. I didn't know why. Something was stopping me.

After a while, Ted went back into the pub and I stepped out of my hiding place and got on the bus home. All I could think about was eating. It was the ONLY thought in my mind. I got off the bus right by the off-licence, Tesco's and the chip shop – one next to the other: an unholy triumvirate of temptation.

I stood outside the chip shop looking mournfully through the window and feeling anger and frustration rising inside me. I wanted to go in there and buy about six packets of saveloy and chips with a side portion of curry sauce, then I wanted to buy bread and butter and wine, and I wanted to swig the wine from the bottle without pouring it into a glass.

The thought of it all thrilled me. The more I could eat and drink, the more I would bury all the anger and frustration inside me. I stood in the cold night air for what seemed like hours, just smelling the vinegar. I wasn't hungry and the smell wasn't making me think 'ooooo…delicious', the smell was making me think 'ooo…here is something that I can use to make myself feel better…here is something that will make the pain go away…not for long, but for a short while, and right now any break from my mad, whirring thoughts will be good.'

"Can I help you, Mary?" asked the lady inside.

Oh God.

The fact that she knew my name made me feel like I'd been shot. How could the lady in the chip shop know my name?

"Everything OK?" she asked.

"Yes," I said, retreating from the alluring smells and warmth. "Everything's fine."

And I knew what I had to do. I had to reach out for help. I pulled my phone out of my pocket. There were lots of missed calls from Ted, and I felt a low pain deep inside me when I saw his name on the screen. Tears started pouring from my eyes as I dialled Liz's number. She should have finished her next class by now. Relief flooded through me when she answered on the second ring.

"Are you alright?" she asked.

"No," I said, bursting into tears. "I feel terrible, I'm messing everything up. I'm standing outside the chip shop and I'm dying to go in, I just want to eat. I've ruined my relationship with Ted and I don't know why. Everything in my life feels completely out of control."

"Well, that's simply not true, is it?" said Liz, calmly. "Everything in your life is not out of control because instead of having chips you rang me. Instead of falling into food as the answer, you reached out, and I'm going to try and help you. I want you to walk back to your flat, go inside, put the kettle on and wait for me to arrive. We're not going to let you sabotage this lovely relationship you've got, and we're not going to let you sabotage your weight loss campaign – we're going to talk this through and sort it out, OK?"

"Yes," I muttered.

"You're just feeling insecure and unworthy, and you're pushing Ted away because your self-esteem is struggling. I could see it all over you tonight. We can sort this out. Go and put the kettle on: I'm on my way."

"Thank you," I said, all tears and snot. "Thank you so much."

5. LIZ IS MY HERO

"*R*ight, young lady: first question – did you get chips?"

"No," I said, in all honesty. I did buy two bottles of wine, just in case, but she didn't ask me about wine, so I kept that to myself.

"Well done, lovely," she said, giving me a huge hug. "I'm very proud of you."

"I don't feel very proud of myself." I burst into tears again. "I've been treating Ted appallingly and I don't know why. What's wrong with me? He's the nicest guy ever. I'm such an idiot, I'm such a loser. Why am I doing this? Look at the state of me? It's not as if men are queuing up to be with me. For God's sake – I'm ridiculous. I don't deserve him."

While I collapsed in floods of tears, Liz stroked my back gently.

"Do you want me to tell you what I think is going on?" she said.

"Yes please," I spluttered through a veil of tears.

"Right. Well, I think all the answers to every question you have are tucked away in what you've just said."

"Are they?"

"Yes, look, what drove you to eat a lot in the first place were your emotional issues, am I right?"

"Yes," I said. That was certainly the reason for my overeating that we identified on the first course. Though I still hadn't explained which emotional issue.

"Now, what we've learned on the course so far is that eating to excess is not the answer. Eating gives you temporary reprieve from your feelings, but it doesn't change them, so there's no point in stuffing yourself full of food in order to bury feelings – the feelings will still be there and you'll get fatter and fatter."

"Yes, I know, and I've been good – I had a breakthrough on the course and learned to completely accept that eating doesn't change anything when it comes to feelings and emotions."

"You've been amazing," confirmed Liz. "Now, let's just think about those feelings and emotions that are all churned up. They are still there. You are learning to live with them, and learning not to suppress them with food, but they haven't gone anywhere. So, what happens is, from time to time, they get the better of you – they rear up and they attack you as sudden panic, anger, frustration or plain madness. I'm the same. I can act in the most obscure of ways when my emotions kick off, or when someone says something, however innocent and benign it may appear on the outside, but for some reason it starts something off in me and I just fall into a whirlwind of confused emotions. Unfortunately, when you feel like that, you often take it out on the person closest to you...as you have...with Ted."

"Yes," I said, feeling calmer all the time at the news that I wasn't bonkers, and what I was going through was something that even Liz herself had struggled with.

"It might be worth talking to someone," she said.

"I'm talking to you."

"No, I mean a psychiatrist...someone trained properly to help you."

"Is that expensive?" I asked. It certainly sounded like it would be.

"No, if you go through your GP, you'll get it on the NHS. You need to be really clear with the GP about how bad you're feeling. Tell him or her everything, and you'll get a referral and should see someone soon," she said. "In the meantime, I want you to follow these instructions if you feel down, concerned or worried." She placed a list of actions to follow on the edge of my desk. "They will help."

"Thank you," I said to Liz, giving her a big hug, as she stood up to leave.

"That's - um - interesting," she said, pointing at the sketch on the wall.

"Er, yes," I said. "A symbol of the more reckless side of my personality."

"Go on..."

"Do you remember that art gallery that we gate-crashed when we met up, soon after the first Fat Club course finished?"

"Oh no, no. Is that the..."

"Yes, it's the Picasso sketch. I ended up having to buy it. Well, mum and dad stepped in to help me out. The auction house was threatening to take me to court if I didn't come up with the money."

"Oh angel," said Liz, enveloping me in a big hug. "Well, it looks good there, anyway."

"So it bloody should. It's worth more than everything else in this flat all put together."

I didn't know whether it was the process of talking that helped me, or whether it was laughing with her about the Picasso print, but I felt better – much better - after she left. I could go and get help. Everything would be OK.

I walked over to the fridge and poured myself a large glass of wine to celebrate. Everything was going to be OK.

6. BUGGER, BUGGER, BUGGER

*W*ell, that didn't go brilliantly. It was hard, in many ways, to work out how it could have gone worse. You know that one glass of wine I had after Liz had left? It turned into two. Yes, I know what you're thinking – two glasses is OK – stop worrying.

Mmmm... I wish!

I had two bloody bottles.

Two bottles.

It was now 5am and I was wide-awake and struggling with the worst hangover in the world. My head was pounding inside my skull, so much so that I didn't want to lift it off the pillow because I was worried that my brain might literally burst through and bounce across the room. I knew I had to get some water or I'd get worse and worse and never get back to sleep again.

OK, here we go... I stepped out of bed and saw my phone lying on the bedside table.

Oh shit. That was when I remembered.

I texted Ted last night. Shit. Shit shit shit. Why did I think it was a good idea to text anyone at 1am? Why didn't I just go to sleep after Liz left? I felt great then – energised and happy. But for some reason I started drinking, and the drinking made the emotions darker and I drank more to cover them... I did everything that I knew I wasn't supposed to do.

I picked up my phone, and the text was there – sitting on the screen, looking up at me:

"What the fuck am in wine and drinking and that stupid woman Michella fuck her. Am in wine."

Oh God. Really? I was sure I used to have some sort of self-preservation that kicked in when I was drunk and stopped me from sending texts like that. When I was young I'd go out to nightclubs and get blind drunk with my friends, but still somehow return home in one piece and without sending absurd texts to men.

I sat down at my desk and looked forlornly at the computer, open on Ted's Facebook page. Oh God. I hadn't messaged him through Facebook as well, had I? I clicked onto Facebook messenger...thankfully I hadn't attempted to contact him. I came back out onto his page.

Then I saw it: "Ted is now friends with Michella Bootle."

Great! He'd befriended her on Facebook.

And that was it. I was off again...my mind spinning and my stomach churning.

I bet he walked her home after the drink last night, and went in for coffee, and snuggled up on the sofa, and perhaps even had sex. I bet they did have sex. I bet it was better sex than he'd ever had with me. Then he climbed out of her bed and headed home, and immediately befriended her on Facebook.

I decided that I, too, would befriend Michella on Facebook. You know what they say – keep your friends close and your enemies closer. Michella was about the biggest enemy a woman could ever have. I would keep her close.

I sent her a friend request, and it gave me the option to add a message, so I tapped out a friendly note: "Hi Mich, it was lovely to meet you last night. I'm really sorry I had to rush off but I felt unwell. I hope you had a good time and look forward to seeing you next week."

Then I stared at the screen like a woman demented. I hit refresh several times. Why wasn't she responding? I decided it must be because she was with Ted. They were in bed together at that very moment. I carried on hitting refresh in a maniacal fashion. Then I saw the piece of paper that Liz left me with last night, and I followed her instructions…

1. Breathe deeply
2. Put two feet firmly on the floor
3. Clear your mind
4. Think about the earth beneath you and the walls in front of you…ground yourself
5. Repeat to yourself that this will pass…everything will be OK

"Everything will be OK," I said. "Everything will be OK." I repeated this until my eyes were closing and my bed was calling. I staggered through the apartment and flopped onto my bed, disgusted with Ted and disgusted with Michella, but calmer… much calmer.

By the time I woke up in the morning, there was a message from Michella: "Lovely to be friends on Facebook, Mary. Thanks so much for the invitation. I only stayed for one drink last night, then my boyfriend picked me up. Really looking forward to seeing you next week… Ted was telling me how madly in love with you he is. X"

7. MAKING IT ALL RIGHT AGAIN

"*I*'m sorry."

Little words that should be easy to say, but are so hard in practice.

I looked into the mirror and said the words again: "I'm sorry."

Christ, now all I had to do was say them to Ted. This was going to be much harder than I thought it would.

I picked up my phone and started pacing around the room. "Come on, Mary – you can do this," I said to myself in the manner of a boxer, revving himself up for the fight of his life. "You can do it, girl. You can do it."

Ah, but I couldn't. I put the phone down.

Oh God, this was so crazy. This man meant the world to me, why couldn't I just pick up the phone and talk to him? Why couldn't I stop this madness? I wanted to be with him. But I couldn't phone him – I was too scared. Too scared he might dump me as soon as he heard my voice.

WhatsApp. That was what I'd do – I'd send a message.

I knew that was wimpy but it was better than doing nothing, and I really wanted to get a message through to him sooner rather than later.

"I'm sorry," I typed into the phone, and hit send before I could change my mind.

"What are you sorry for?" he replied straight away.

"I'm sorry for everything. I'm sorry I have been so horrible to you, I'm sorry I rushed out last night, I'm sorry for sending a horrible text. I'm really, really sorry. Ted – I'm sorry you're not here in my arms right now. I'm just sorry."

Tears were in my eyes as I hit the send button.

"Are you at home?" he texted back.

"Yes," I replied.

"I'm on my way, if that's OK," he replied.

"Yes, of course it is!" I messaged back, and it felt like the greatest day ever.

I sat back and smiled to myself. Ted was coming over. Then I realised TED WAS COMING OVER. The flat looked a mess.

I threw myself into a tidying and cleaning routine with terrifying and reckless speed, running around with furniture polish and a cloth and dragging the vacuum cleaner across the carpets and the wooden floors.

Next it was time for me to sort myself out. I washed quickly, shaving every part of my body that he was likely to come into contact with, and covering myself in the body lotion that I knew he loved the smell of. Then I dressed in casual clothes so it didn't look as if I'd just charged around and prepared myself for him. I wanted to look casual but beautiful…natural and glamorous all at the same time. I put on lipstick (because I didn't want to look THAT natural) and brushed my hair. The doorbell went and I looked in the mirror. Not too bad, actually, even if I said so myself.

Ted certainly seemed to think I looked OK. He charged in and grabbed me, sweeping me up into his arms; hugging and kissing me and I burst into tears. It felt like the most wonderful thing ever to happen, better, even, than when we first got together.

"Liz explained to me how bad you were feeling, and that you were confused and guilty. I understand," he said.

"But what about that text I sent?"

"I didn't get a text," he replied.

"Oh, perhaps I didn't actually send it," I said. "Phew – it didn't make any sense anyway so that's OK."

Ted was looking right into my eyes. "I was going to write 'I love you' in rose petals on the ground outside your door," he said. "I was trying to think of the most romantic thing to do. I didn't know what to do… I'm not very good at this stuff."

"You're amazing at this stuff," I said, kissing his neck.

"Bed," he replied, practically dragging me through to the bedroom and tearing at my clothes. I could feel his hands shaking as he pulled my bra straps down and cupped my breasts tenderly. He was just about to pull my trousers down and begin doing what a man and a woman do when they're on their own and feeling randy, when he stopped suddenly.

"I love you," he said. "I really love you."

"I love you too," I replied.

And after that we fell into a deep silence, punctuated only by gentle moans from me and occasional growls from him. It was all marvellous, dear reader, bloody marvellous.

8. MEETING THE FAMILY

*A*fter our initial bed-centred reunion, I explained everything to Ted, and – to his credit – he didn't judge or criticise or complain, he listened to what I had to say, nodded and told me he loved me and not to worry.

I explained all about what happened when Liz came round and he said he was proud of me for reaching out for help, but he really wished it had been him that I'd turned to. That was a good point... I didn't know why I hadn't. Perhaps Ted meant too much for me to make myself vulnerable and confess my emotions to him, or perhaps it was just that Liz had always told us to call her if we were in distress, so that was the call I made. Either way, Ted and I reached a really happy place. Everyone at Fat Club was delighted last week when I said that the two of us were completely back together and happier than ever. In fact, things were so great that Ted was taking me to visit his mum and dad. It felt like a huge move.

Oh, and – by the way – I went to see my GP and she was brilliant. She is going to try and get me an urgent appointment with a therapist who'll be able to help me deal with all my issues. I was feeling better and more confident than ever. Except for today. I wasn't feeling wildly confident today because of the whole 'meet the parents' thing...

What if they really hated me? They might think I wasn't good enough for their precious son and the truth was – they'd probably be right.

Ted knocked on the door of their lovely semi-detached in Esher. It was a nice-looking house on a tree-lined street...very suburban, but very neat and tidy.

Ted let himself in through the front door and we wandered into the sitting room, where I met Ted's mum and sister. They jumped up when we walked in and rushed over to embrace Ted and shake my hand. They were both unnervingly slender and well-dressed. His mum had a real warmth about her. His sister – not so much – she was a little sour, and gave me the feeling, as she slowly looked me up and down, that she didn't like me at all.

"This is Mary," said Ted, and his mum grabbed me in a tight embrace. I was (not for the first time) embarrassed to be so large. The woman could barely get her arms around me. She felt so little and delicate. I experienced a longing to be the same way.

His sister smiled a half-smile. "Really nice to meet you," she said. "Ted has told us ALL about you, ALL the time. He never stops talking about you, to be honest. It's quite nauseating."

"Oy!" said Ted, smacking his sister.

"You're both so tiny," I said. "I'm very envious of how you keep so thin."

"You need to eat less," said his sister, bluntly. "Like Ted – he needs to eat a lot less too."

There was a horrible silence between us that no one really knew how to fill.

I felt the need to keep things light so I prodded Ted in the stomach affectionately. "Well, we certainly know who eats all the pies in this house, don't we?" I said.

I didn't think the comment per se was particularly offensive...it was designed to lift the mood and add some joviality, but what made the comment offensive, and wholly inappropriate was that – exactly as I said it – Ted's dad walked into the room. I say walked, what I mean was waddled. Ted's dad was huge. Massive. He was probably the same size as Ted and me together.

"Someone talking about me?" asked his dad. "Someone saying that I eat all the pies?"

Shit. "No," I said. "Of course not. Definitely not. God, I'm sorry – I was talking about Ted."

"Thanks a lot," said Ted.

"No, I mean – you're a lot bigger than your mum and sister. I was only trying to be nice to your mum and sister. I'm sorry."

Ted's dad shoehorned himself into a large armchair which suddenly looked tiny beneath his massive girth.

His mum went over and removed his shoes, then pulled out the bottom part of the chair which formed a foot-rest. She lifted his legs and put them onto it. Ted's dad stared into space. I decided I didn't like him very much. Not just because I'd inadvertently insulted him, but because he seemed so different from Ted's mum. He seemed distracted and uncommunicative. The opposite to my smiley, happy, chatty Ted.

"I'm sorry if that seemed offensive," I said. "I didn't see you coming, I was talking about…"

"Didn't see him coming," said Sian, Ted's sister. "How could you not see him coming? Look at the size of him."

"Oh God – they all hate me. They all hate me so much," I said to Ted, later that night when we were curled up in my bed, recalling the day with wine and slices of melon (I have a theory that fruit cancels out the calories in wine).

"No, they don't – that's just the way they are. Mum thought you were wonderful and she's the only one who counts. Dad is just miserable, and my sister is madly jealous of any woman who comes anywhere near me so you're never going to have a chance with her, but Mum – Mum is special, she's lovely, kind and wonderful and really looks after the family. She's the only one who matters, and she thinks you're great."

"Thank you," I said, and felt much better about everything.

9. SEAT BELT TRAUMAS

"Cheer up, sunshine, it might never happen."

Dave was standing in his garden looking dishevelled and filthy and absolutely bloody gorgeous. How is it that some men look better the less care they take of themselves? If Dave lived in a bin for a week he'd look like a bloody film star. He'd just get more manly and more desirable as he got stubblier and dirtier. The man reeked of masculinity. It was very distracting.

"It has already happened," I said. "I've booked my first ever driving lesson for this morning and I'm dreading it."

"Why?" asked Dave.

"Because I need to learn to drive."

"No, not – why have you booked a lesson. I meant – why are you dreading it? Learning to drive is a great thing to do."

"Because I'll be rubbish and probably crash the car and kill us all."

"No you won't – driving's easy," said Dave. "Just look around at all the idiots who can drive. If they can do it, so can you. I can even drive drunk, so it can't be that difficult."

"Ha ha," I replied.

"No, I really can," said Dave. "I did last night. Well, I say I did – I don't remember doing it, but I must have because the car is here."

"Really? You really drove home completely drunk?"

"Yep." There was a strange pride in his voice.

"You could have killed yourself." I was eager not to encourage or celebrate his reckless behaviour.

"But I didn't," he said proudly. "There's not a scratch on me."

"You could have hurt someone."

"But I didn't. I don't think so anyway. Hard to know for sure, but I don't think so or the police would have been round."

"It's not funny," I said. "Lots of people are killed by drink drivers. It's not a laughing matter at all."

"OK, killjoy, calm down. How am I supposed to get home after a few pints if I don't drive?"

"Er – walk? Get a cab? Get a train? Get a bus? Lots of options."

"I was too drunk to walk," said Dave. "Too drunk for all of those things. That's why I drove. Anyway, I'm going to bed. Good luck in your lesson. And remember – if I can do it drunk, it can't be that hard."

"No, indeed," I responded, and Dave went staggering back into his house, weaving across his small patio and stumbling through his front door.

A couple of minutes after Dave's manly frame had disappeared from view, a small yellow car appeared on the horizon, with 'Sunnyside Driving' plastered across the sides and with ridiculous primroses on the bonnet and eyelashes on the front lights. No one would be able to miss me in this thing...assuming I could get into it: my arse was bigger than the boot.

"Is it Mary?" asked the driving instructor, waving to me through the open window. He looked like he was going for his first day as a clerk at a suburban branch of Barclays. He was wearing a yellow tie to match the car and a V-neck jumper with a jacket over the top. He stepped out of the car looking slightly nervous. I noticed that his trousers were a fraction too tight...like school trousers he'd grown out of but his mum hadn't replaced.

"Yes, I'm Mary." I lifted myself off the small wall.

Standing up and sitting down are two of the things I find hardest to do as a fatty. I had to use my hands to lever myself off the wall, and as I leaned forward, my protruding stomach got in the way. The other thing I hate is doing my shoelaces. The agony of leaning over to do anything, anything at all, when you're heavy cannot be overstated. I feel a wave of nausea and sickness wash through me whenever I bend over, as if my stomach is pushing up against all my internal organs and stopping them from working properly.

I waddled towards the car and the driving instructor shook my hand and told me to get into the passenger seat.

"We'll head out to a disused shopping centre car park and have a chat and get started," he said. "That way there'll be no pressure and no one to see you. OK?"

"OK," I said and felt massively relieved. The guy seemed calm and in control, and I liked the idea of going to learn in an old disused car park rather than on the road. Nothing could go wrong if I was miles from other people and cars. Could it?

I sat down heavily in the seat and the whole car felt like it had dropped beneath me – like a fat kid sitting on the see-saw.

"Seat belt on then," he said.

Ah.

I pulled the seat belt as slowly as I could, hoping that it was long enough to go round me, but it jolted to a stop a considerable way short. Damn. I pulled again, ever so slowly in case the reason it had stopped was because it had got caught up or triggered the stop mechanism, but – no – it had stopped because that was the end of it. The seat belt didn't get any longer. I was too fat for the seat belt. It was mortifying.

"All done up?" asked the driving instructor, unaware of the crushing few seconds I'd just endured.

"Yes," I replied, tucking the seat belt down beside my thigh, and pretending it was done up.

"OK, I want you to watch me as I drive, then we'll be talking about it when we get to the car park. See how the first thing I do is to put the key into the ignition and turn it." He did this and the car immediately started beeping like we were out of petrol or something.

"Ah, that beeping is to say that the seat belts aren't done up. Can you check yours is properly clicked in," he said.

Oh hell. This is horrible.

"Yep, all clicked in," I replied. But I could see that this strategy wasn't going to get me very far. He was going to start investigating.

"Are you sure?" he asked.

"Yes, all fine. Just drive."

"I can't drive while the emergency warning light's on. It means one of the seat belts isn't done up properly and that could be extremely dangerous."

Oh for God's sake, man.

"We're not travelling far though, are we? Let's just go," I said.

But Mr Health & Safety was out of the car and over to my side of the car to examine the seat belt situation.

"Oh it's not done up at all!" he said. "Look, can you see? It's not plugged in, that's what the problem is."

Silly me.

Then he started pulling it and fiddling with the seat belt container, trying to work out why the seat belt wouldn't go in and end the interminable bleeping that was still belting away inside the little car.

"It seems shorter this side than the other, I can't get enough of it to come out," he said, baffled. Bless him. Could he not see that I was fucking huge and that it simply wasn't big enough to go round me? We could blame the seat belt all we wanted, but the truth was that I was so large that a conventional seat belt wouldn't go round me. It wasn't the first time this had happened, and I was sure it wouldn't be the last, but it was still mortifying.

I could see my poor, dear driving instructor suddenly working out what had happened. I could see it in his body language as he pulled himself up short, and stood with his hands on his hips, looking down. I also sensed that this was probably the worst thing that had ever happened to him. It was like he felt personally responsible for the fact that the seat belt didn't work, even though it was entirely my fault.

He had no idea what to do. On one hand there was his absolute horror of having to tell me that I was too fat for his seat belt; on the other hand, there was his absolute horror of breaking any of the rules of the road – so he didn't want to drive off with me unable to wear a seat belt. If he'd had any more hands, I imagined that on the third one there would be the issue of him not wanting to lose my business. The invisible third hand won, he got back into his side of the car and off we went, in search of an empty car park so that the fat girl could drive around without killing anyone.

When we reached the car park there were children playing football at the far side of it.

"Be careful," the instructor screamed out of the window. "Learner driver here…"

"I'll be fine," I told him, but the instructor didn't look as if he thought it was going to be at all fine. He was gripping onto the sides of the door as he encouraged me to look in my mirror before moving off, then he told me to keep looking in the mirror. "It's the most important thing," he said, though I didn't think that looking behind me could be that important, could it? I felt I was using the mirror so much that I was looking backwards more than I was looking forwards. And all the while, the beeping noise was going on, driving me nuts as I tried to concentrate on driving in a straight line while looking in the mirror. It seemed unlikely I was going to be a natural at driving.

10. DODGY DRIVING AND AN ANGRY POLICEMAN

"*I* could easily teach you to drive," said Dave. "Easily."

I was sitting on the top step with my head in my hands, shaking my head forlornly.

"Don't worry about the driving instructor," he added. "Really, it's easy."

"But everything went wrong, Dave. I mean EVERYTHING. I couldn't get the fucking seat belt on, then my feet wouldn't touch the pedals unless I had the seat all the way forward and then it was so far forward that my stomach was in the way when I tried to reach down to put the key in the ignition. It was all an embarrassing disaster. I'm not cut out for driving. I don't know what I am cut out for, all I know is that it's not driving."

"Yes you are, everyone can drive. You can drive, I can teach you to drive – driving is easy. You know what, mate, I'm not great at much: I can get girls to drop their knickers at my door and I can drive. There's no question that I can teach you to drive, so get in the seat and let's get going."

Dave insisted that I needed to be in the driving seat, and that we weren't going to a deserted car park. "We'll just get going, everything will be fine," he insisted. He was an absolute darling to make the effort to teach me, but to be honest, I didn't hold out great deal of hope. In fact, ignore that, I didn't hold out any hope at all.

The good news was, Dave had no complicated beeping situation going on and no lights that flash when I failed to connect the seat belt.

"OK, what do I do first?" I asked.

"We need to get going, sweetheart," he said. "Put the key in ignition and let's get this baby moving."

His was an altogether less sophisticated an approach to the one I'd endured with the driving instructor.

"Turn the key then." I did as I was told and edged the car forward on Dave's command, juddering and faltering as it hopped along like a bunny rabbit.

"OK," said Dave. "So we're moving, but now can we drive it so it's like a car and not like a fucking woodland creature."

"OK, how do I do that?"

"Didn't the driving instructor tell you?"

"No, we didn't get that far."

"How far did you get then?" he asked. "I mean – if driving for a bit in a straight line wasn't touched upon, what exactly were you doing?"

"We were doing things like mirror, signal, manoeuvre," I said.

"Oh yes, yes, yes you need to do that. I forgot about all that stuff. Yes, do that as well…before you start driving around."

"OK." I was really starting to wonder now whether Dave was absolutely the right person to be teaching me to drive.

Still, we set off, with me trying to remember everything the driving instructor said about mirror, signal, manoeuvre, and how to proceed cautiously. I kept looking in the mirror to make sure cyclists weren't passing and made sure I knew what cars were behind me. Dave seemed strangely unaware of these simple rules of the road.

One thing I was really struggling with was driving a different car to the one the previous day. I didn't know how you were supposed to remember how much force to use in different cars. The driving instructor's car was somehow slower, everything took a little longer. It meant that when I turned the wheel in Dave's car with the sort of force I used in the instructor's, the car went up and onto the pavement until I brought it to a juddering halt within inches of a lamppost.

"Well." Dave grabbed the steering wheel and redirected it back onto the road. "That wasn't great. And just as I was starting to think you were getting the hang of it. And slow down, for goodness' sake, why are you going so fast? It's like being in a car with Lewis Hamilton."

"OK, I'll try," I said, once firmly back on solid ground and driving at a sensible speed.

"You're still going too fast; you have to slow down," said Dave. "Slow right down... You need to slow down, Mary."

"I am going slowly."

"No, you're not," said Dave. We approached a zebra crossing as someone walked out, so I slammed on the brakes, sending both of us flying forward so we had to put our hands out to stop ourselves careering through the windscreen. I had no seat belt on because I was terrifyingly fat, and Dave had no seat belt on out of some inexplicable sympathy with me (he'd said, "I won't wear one either then." A decision he was coming to bitterly regret).

"What was that for?" said Dave with considerable aggression. "I told you to slow down earlier. You can't just drive full pelt and put your brakes on at the last minute, it's not fair on the drivers behind you and it's not fair to those walking across the zebra crossing. Also, it's not fair to me. I'm a bloody nervous wreck here, doll face. Now slow down."

"OK, OK."

"Go on then, the traffic is waiting behind."

I wasn't very good at starting yet, so I put my foot flat down on the pedal and the car leaped forward.

"Bring the car to the side of the road," Dave said, in measured tones. He sounded quite scared now.

"Sorry?"

"I want you to park the car at the side of the road."

Parking was something we hadn't done yet, so I brought the car to an emergency stop.

"Not in the middle of the road," said Dave, pointing towards the curb while holding his head in the other hand.

"I don't really know about bringing the car into the curb," I replied. "If you remember, you're supposed to be teaching me how to do all this stuff."

"OK, turn the steering wheel towards the curb, put your foot down on the accelerator gently and it will go towards the curb... It's not that hard."

"OK, I'll give it a go."

Anyway, that was how we ended up with the car half on the pavement and half on the road, and Dave instructing me to reverse off the pavement back into the road.

"I've never done reversing before," I said. "Where is the reverse button?"

"Oh God," he said, as he began to talk me through the process of reversing, telling me to put my foot down on the clutch as he moved the gear stick to reverse. I then put my foot down on the accelerator in a manner that I believed to be gentle, but was clearly more aggressive than it should have been. The car flew back. I braked suddenly and Dave and I went shooting forward. I bashed my head on the steering wheel which emitted a loud beep.

"Don't beep the horn," he said. "You're bringing enough attention to us as it is."

"I didn't beep the horn," I said. "My head hit the horn when I went flying in my seat."

"OK then, well you better move us forward a bit, you're sticking out into the road and the cars can't get past."

I suppose it was inevitable, really, but the next car to come along was a police car. "For the love of Christ," said Dave, as the panda car pulled alongside me and the officer wound down his window. "Everything OK?" The police officer gave a dramatic raise of his eyebrows as he spoke, indicating that, to his mind at least, things were far from OK.

"I'm sorry, officer, I'm learning to drive," I said. "It's harder than it looks, isn't it?"

"Indeed it is," said the officer. "For starters you should have L-plates on the car."

"I forgot to put them on," said Dave. "I will put them on next time we come out."

The officer didn't look convinced, but he could see we were in a perilous situation, and he needed to leave us so I could remove the car from its position, sitting diagonally across the road. So he just nodded and said, "Make sure you do."

And at this stage – I promise you – everything was OK. All we had to do was get out of the ridiculous position I'd got us into, and continue on our journey. But Dave, being Dave, couldn't let it lie like that...

"Dickhead," he said, thinking the policeman was out of earshot. But the policeman wasn't out of earshot. He reversed the car back alongside my car and looked over at Dave. "Sorry, did you say something?" he asked.

And this was when I made the biggest cock-up ever. I figured it would be good to diffuse the situation with a light-hearted joke. Big mistake.

"Honestly, officer, he had three pints at lunchtime – you can't talk to him when he's like this." I looked over at Dave and nudged him playfully.

"She's joking," he said plaintively.

"Of course I'm joking." I looked back at the policeman who was getting out of his car and coming round to open the door.

"Get out," he instructed, all of the gentleness having gone from his voice.

"OK, officer." I stepped out of the car.

"Why aren't you wearing your seat belt?"

"I was," I lied. "I took it off when you came up alongside us."

"OK, you get out of the car too," he said to Dave. "And blow into this..."

The police officer handed Dave a breathalyser.

"I'm not blowing into that," said Dave. "Not without my lawyer present."

"Dave, just blow into it," I said. Then I turned to the officer: "Really, I was just joking, this is getting way out of hand... It was a little joke."

"It wasn't funny. Drink-driving is serious."

"You'll have to take me to the station, I'm not blowing into that bag," said Dave. The policeman was getting very agitated, and everyone was getting angry and cross with one another.

"Mary, can you call my lawyer on this number..."

He handed me a piece of paper with 'I can't blow into that thing, I've been drinking all morning,' written on it. What the hell were we supposed to do now?

"I was joking," I said to the officer. "This is going to look ridiculous when it all goes to court and I say I was making a little joke and you took it way too seriously. The police have a bad enough reputation for being hard-headed at the best of times. I'm really sorry I made a joke...it was in poor taste. I promise I'll never make a joke like that again."

"OK, OK," said the police officer. He turned to Dave: "Make sure you get those L-plates."

"I will," said Dave, and the officer drove off.

"Bloody hell!" I walked towards Dave. "You were drinking this morning?"

"Yes." He wrapped his arms around me as we clung to one another in relief.

"But you can't drink drive."

"I didn't drink drive. You were driving."

"Oh, bloody hell," I said. "You're such an idiot."

Behind us there was traffic chaos. Cars were beeping and drivers had got out and were standing on the road shouting at us to "move the f**king car."

"I better move it." I extracted myself from Dave's arms...he'd been holding on to me way longer than I'd expected him to.

We got into the car. I reversed out and nearly hit three people, Dave held his head in his hands and people all around us shouted angrily.

. . .

Later that night, Ted phoned. He'd been due to come round for the evening, but said he wasn't feeling well.

"Oh no, sorry about that," I said.

"What did you do today?" he asked.

"Nothing much." I couldn't possibly tell him about the driving lesson. He'd have a fit if he thought I'd done a driving lesson with a drunk bloke.

"See anyone?" he asked.

I decided not to mention Downstairs Dave.

"No," I said. "I just hung around at home and did some chores. How about you?"

"I have to go," he said, and he disappeared from the line.

Poor thing, he sounded really unwell.

11. HUGGING DAVE

I woke in the morning to a text from Ted.

"Are you awake?" it said.

"Yes," I replied.

A minute later my phone rang.

"This is awkward," he said. "It's awkward and it's fucking awful."

"What's happened?"

"I know that you and Dave are having an affair," he said. "Don't deny it because I know for sure."

I sat up in bed. "What the hell are you talking about? Of course I'm not having an affair with him or anyone else – I'm in love with you."

"My sister saw you," he said.

"She didn't."

"She did."

"No, she didn't, because I'm not having an affair with him. It must have been someone else. To be honest, Ted, I've seen a lot of women go in and out of his flat – it could be any one of them."

"Don't lie, Mary," he said, and I could hear how deadly serious he was.

"Ted, I promise you, I'm not having an affair with Dave. I don't know how to make it any clearer."

"Then explain this," he said, and my phone bleeped to tell me there was a text. I went into my texts and retrieve one from Ted. It consisted of a picture...of Dave and me with our arms wrapped round each other, caught up in a huge hug. Oh God. It looked really dodgy.

"Have you got it?" asked Ted.

"Yes."

"You told me you'd spent all your time in the house doing chores, so you're lying to me. I can only assume you lied because you're seeing Dave. Thanks very much."

"No, no, it's not like that," I tried.

"So, you didn't lie to me?"

"Well, yes I did, but not because I'm having an affair. I lied because Dave gave me a driving lesson and I discovered afterwards – after the police stopped us, but that's another story – I discovered afterwards that he'd been drinking all morning. Look, Dave's an idiot and I shouldn't have got him to teach me to drive, but he offered and I really want to learn."

"Why didn't you ask me?" said Ted. "Why do you always turn to other people for help?"

"Because I don't want to look an idiot in front of you."

"And it doesn't look like much driving's going on in the picture... you've obviously been kissing him."

"No. I hugged him in relief because the police didn't arrest him."

"This is all ridiculous," said Ted. "I'm going now."

"No, don't go," I said. "Ted, I love you. This is all a silly mix-up."

But it was too late. Ted had gone and I was left holding my phone on which there was a picture of Dave and me in an embrace. Oh God. There was only one woman to call at a time like this.

I dialled Charlie's number. Luckily, she was in and answered straight away.

"Send me the picture," she told me, when I'd explained my predicament.

"Mmmm...that's not great," she said. "What are you going to do?"

"I've no idea," I said. "That's why I'm calling you."

"Probably time for an old-fashioned committee meeting, don't you think?"

"Blimey, we haven't done one of those for ages."

We always used to call a committee meeting if one of us was struggling with something (usually involving a man). All the girls would descend on the stricken woman's house and they would jointly work out what was the best course of action.

"Your place, tonight at 6pm, I'll let the girls know. See you later."

See – I told you Charlie would be the right person to talk to.

There was wine, there were low-calorie, fat-free nibbles, and fresh flowers filled the room with a soft, rose scent. I was all prepared, but feeling dreadful. I really didn't want to lose Ted. Charlie nodded her approval as she surveyed the scene and helped herself to a cheese puff.

"Don't worry, angel, we'll sort this out," she said.

"I hope so. I'm such an idiot."

I put some music on and read through the agenda I prepared in advance of this key tactical and strategic meeting.

It was headed 'operation MATT' (Mary and Ted together), followed by the list of people who'd be there later: me, Charlie, Janice and Veronica from Fat Club, and Sandra the beautician whose arms I cried in when I bumped into her on the High Street that afternoon. To be honest, I think she was just relieved that she hadn't received a legal letter after she'd turned my skin the colour of boiled beetroot. Anything else was a bonus.

1. Convince Ted that Mary still likes him
2. Convince Ted that Mary is trustworthy, and that nothing happened with Downstairs Dave
3. Approach Ted's sister?
4. Infiltrate Ted's friend group to convince them that Ted and Mary should be together
5. Get Ted and Mary together whenever possible
6. Drop lots of hints to Ted about how great the two of them are together

Obviously at the end there would be time for Any Other Business, and there would be someone taking notes and making sure that all the things talked about were implemented. There would be follow-up meetings, more strategising, and regular catch-ups. It wasn't exactly the United Nations, but it wasn't far off.

The girls began to arrive, streaming into my house, taking a glass of wine and chatting amiably while we all collected in the front room. Madonna sang out from the stereo as hands disappeared into bowls of low-fat crisps, and glasses were replenished.

"Right, if everyone could take a seat, we will begin," said Charlie, taking the lead and addressing the assembled guests. "We have a terrible situation on our hands. Our lovely Mary has managed to behave like a giant buffoon, and spend time in the company of Downstairs Dave, henceforth to be referred to as Double D. Their liaison has come to Ted's knowledge, and he has told Mary that he is unhappy. A small argument ensued and now Mary and Ted have split up. The purpose of today's meeting is to work out how to get them back together again."

"What have you done so far?" asked Sandra, as she finished her wine and laid her glass on the table.

I reached out to refill her glass. "I haven't really done anything," I confessed. "I don't really know what to do."

"Tell us what happened," she said.

"Well, Dave offered to teach me to drive, I thought it would be a really good idea, because the day before I'd had a terrible driving lesson. Dave said he was a good teacher. Turns out he is a really crap teacher and a really crap driver, the whole thing was a disaster. He nearly went into shock when I mounted the curb, and he was rude to a police officer, then I told the police officer that he was drunk, then he refused to blow into the breathalyser because it turns out he *was* drunk, then we were so relieved when the policeman went away that we hugged. I didn't realise that Ted sister had seen me and taken a picture which she showed to Ted."

"Oh," said Sandra. "What a pickle. And where were baby Kate and baby William when all this was going on?"

"Oh don't worry about them. They were fine. With the Nanny," I said. I'd completely forgotten about that ridiculous story I told.

"A man not trusting the mother of his new-born twins. Terrible," continued Sandra.

"Nope, all good. Not to worry. Let's move on."

"What twins?" asked Charlie.

"No twins. Just the need to get Ted back on side."

"For what it's worth, I think his sister is a bitch," said Veronica. "I mean – really? That's such a tosser-ish thing to do."

"It is," said Charlie. "His sister knows nothing about what's going on and decides to intervene. She just doesn't like Mary."

"But I can't slag off the sister to Ted, the two of them are very close, and he is sure that his sister was simply acting in his best interests," I explained.

"OK," said Janice. "The first question, then, what have you said to Ted so far?"

"I told him the truth," I replied, smiling inwardly with pride. I'm the sort of person who always manages to make a mountain out of a molehill...the sort of person who opens her mouth and makes everything 50 times worse. But, on this occasion, I didn't seem to have done that. I'd just told the truth.

"And what did Ted say?"

"He was sceptical. He didn't understand why I'd lied originally about it...which I hadn't...I just didn't tell him the whole truth which, as everyone knows, is different from lying."

"OK, OK," said Charlie. "Enough of what has happened. What are we going to do to put it all right again? Has everyone got an agenda? Let's bring this meeting to order."

There was a shuffling sound as everyone picked up their papers.

"OK, first item on the agenda – convince Ted that Mary still likes him. How are we going to do that?"

"I'm friends with him on Facebook," said Janice. "I could send him a note on there. I could just say that I'm checking he's OK, and that

I'm sorry that he and Mary have split up, because I know how much she loves him."

"Good. Excellent. Anyone else?"

"I'll talk to him at Fat Club," said Veronica. "I'll pull him aside and make sure he knows how much she likes him."

"Good." Charlie struck off item one on her agenda. "Now, what's next?"

"Convince Ted that nothing happened with Downstairs Dave," said Janice. "Well, I can do that when I chat to him on Facebook. We don't want too many people approaching him, he might suspect that it's all planned."

"He'll never suspect that we have a bloody working party set up though, will he. Men would never think of doing something like this," said Sandra with a snort. Oh God, she was very drunk. "You know what we should do – get Downstairs Dave to join us. Maybe he'll be able to give us a man's perspective on the whole thing? Or perhaps he'll offer to talk to Ted."

"No, I don't want him talking to Ted," I said.

"Might not be a bad idea to have a male point of view, though," offered Charlie. "I mean – if we just invite him up for a glass of wine and pick his brains for 15 minutes, that would be OK, wouldn't it?"

"I guess so." I wasn't wholly convinced that we needed a male point of view, and I didn't feel great about DD – the cause of all the anguish – being in my flat, but it was decided that he really should contribute to the meeting, so Charlie rushed off to find him and I pondered the situation.

"What if Ted finds that he was here?" I said. "I mean – this could make everything worse."

"If he finds out that DD is here, just tell him that you invited him so you could get a male point of view at the planning evening."

"Yes, but then I'll have to tell him about the planning evening. He'll think I've lost my mind if he knows about what's happening tonight."

"Good point," Janice conceded. "He can't know about any of this or he'll have you carted off to a mental home."

On that note, Downstairs Dave walked into the room and there was an audible sigh as all the women swooned in his wake. He did look lovely…really sexy and dishevelled as always. I finished my glass of wine and steadied myself by gripping hold of the mantelpiece as he leaned over and planted a kiss on my cheek. Well, I say 'cheek', but I turned round suddenly and he caught me on the lips by mistake (yes – mistake!), and there was another audible sigh from the girls in the room as they all contemplated the idea of being kissed by Dave…he really was a spectacularly good-looking man.

"You need to help us," said Charlie, as Dave took handfuls of peanuts and rocketed them into his mouth by slapping his hand up against his lips. "We need to get Mary and Ted back together."

"The fat guy?" said Dave, looking at me.

"Yes."

"Cool. He seems nice. Why don't you tell him you want to go out with him?"

"Well, we were going out together, then he saw me with you, when you were giving me a driving lesson, and he thought something was going on with us, so the relationship ended."

"He thought something was going on with us? With you and me? Really? That's so funny."

"Yes, his sister saw us. Do you remember when the policeman left and we had a hug? She got the wrong idea, told him and he thinks we're having an affair."

"Just tell him we're not," he said. "Just keep saying it…every time you see him. Don't play silly games and get your friends to drop hints – just tell him the truth. Be honest and straightforward. You haven't done anything wrong."

We all looked shell-shocked. Dave leaned over and picked up my phone, playing with it as he talked.

"But we've got a complicated plan."

"You don't need a complicated plan – just tell him the truth."

Just tell him? Really? It couldn't be that simple?

12. ROSE PETALS ON THE BREEZE

*S*o...once again I was sitting at home wondering how to apologise to Ted. It was becoming quite a regular thing in my life. This time I felt like I had to phone him, rather than text. It would be wrong to text after the trouble I'd caused, so I picked up my mobile. I'd been thinking about this all night...since the meeting when Dave was so adamant that I should talk and not play games.

"Hello," he said, all jolly. "Cheered up now?"

"No," I said, miserably. "Why would I have cheered up?"

"Have you been outside today?" he asked.

"No, I haven't. Look, Ted. I really love you. I don't want us to split up."

"Where are you?" he asked. "I mean – have you left the house yet?"

"No," I replied. "I'm still in my pyjamas... I can't face work."

"Open the front door."

"Why?"

"Just do it," he said.

I walked up to the door and swung it open, and there, in front of my house was 'I love you' written out in rose petals., all held down with tiny white stones

"Oh God," I said. "That's so lovely. Oh Ted, that must have taken you ages. Why did you do that? I thought you hated me. You thought I was having an affair with Dave."

"I don't hate you. Of course I don't hate you. I just didn't understand what was going on. It's like you push me away and I think you want space, then as soon as I give it to you, you think I want to leave, then you're hugging men in the street. I didn't know what's going on.

"Then Dave called me yesterday night. He told me he'd taken my number out of your phone when he was at the meeting. He told me what happened. He also told me about how upset you were and about you gathering all your friends together. Turns out he's a pretty decent guy. I'm sorry I didn't believe you. It's just – you know – I was hurt and scared. I don't want to lose you. You don't make it easy, Mary Brown."

"I don't want to lose you." I bent down to gather up some of the rose petals.

"I love you," he said. "I'll always love you."

And every care in the world drifted away on the breeze, followed by dozens of pale pink rose petals.

"Come round," I said.

"I'm on my way," he replied.

13. THE TRUTH AT LAST

*T*ed was clearly able to move at a speed which belied his size. It was minutes before he was running up my pathway and sweeping me into his arms. I was dying to relax and have a gorgeous evening with him. But I knew there were things I needed to tell him, things that he needed to know in order to understand why I behave the way do.

Ted tried to lead me straight into the bedroom when he walked into the flat. I had to stop him and pull him into the sitting room.

"I want to talk to you," I explained.

"We can talk in the bedroom."

"Not this time."

I sat him down on the sofa, and perched next to him…not draped all over him as I usually was, but with my legs tucked up to my chest and my arms wrapped round them. Kind of foetal position, to be honest.

"I want to tell you about what happened to me," I said. "I think it will help, and I want to share it with you."

"OK," he said, reaching over to touch my shoulder in a supportive way. I'm immediately thrown back to when I first met Ted at Fat Club and he reached out to touch me and offer comfort when I was talking about my issues infant of the group. On that occasion I had gone bright red. This time I took his hand before he could pull it away, and held it tightly.

"I was a gymnast when I was younger, as you know. It's a tough sport at the best of times: it's not like other sports in which you train in the week and play at the weekend. Gymnastics is all about the training. You train for months for one competition. There are only one or two big competitions a year, and the Olympics and Commonwealth Games every four years. The rest of the time you're training...and hoping that you don't get injured. Avoiding injury is a crucial part of being good at an Olympic sport. The history of the Games is littered with the broken dreams of gymnasts...stars who got injured at the wrong time and never got to compete. Just think about it - the competitive life of a gymnast is short, and the Games are every four years. It's hard to be at exactly the right age, and at the peak of your performance to win that elusive gold medal. Gymnasts who do it more than once are super-heroes.

"Anyway, sorry, I'm getting a bit distracted. The issue is that staying injury-free is vital, so we have regular check-ups with the medical staff and everything is monitored to check we're in the best shape.

"I went in to see the doctor one day, when I was around 15, and our regular doc wasn't there. There was a male doctor sitting there. I smiled at him, explained that my Achilles heel hurt and he told me to take off my t-shirt."

"Your t-shirt? To fix your ankle?"

"Oh, he made up some rubbish about needing to check my alignment. That also involved him touching me everywhere..."

I started crying at that point, as Ted wrapped his arms around me.

"It was awful and terrifying, and I didn't know what to do. I could have screamed but it felt like my voice had been stolen by fear. Anyway, who would have believed a young girl over a middle-aged doctor? So I lay there and let him touch me. Then he undressed and I panicked. I tried to get away, but he was so much stronger.

"I remember it all so clearly. The gymnasts in the main hall were warming up, and we had this routine we did to the Star Wars music, and I could hear the music playing as held me down and raped me. And I never told anyone. Not anyone."

"Oh Christ, Mary. We need to go and find this guy. Let me spend half an hour with him."

"No, he died years ago. But what he did is always there. It's there in lots of different ways. Even when I hear that damn music I feel threatened. It's awful. And I never brought him to justice. I feel so bad about that. He might have gone on to do the same thing to hundreds of gymnasts because I didn't speak out."

"That's not a helpful way to think, angel. You did your best to cope in an incredibly difficult situation."

"I gave up gymnastics soon afterwards and never kept in contact with any of my old gym friends. Mum and dad never understood why I gave up. No-one did. I coped with it all by eating. But not really coping, if you know what I mean - just surviving by pushing down the pain and guilt with food, and never quite trusting people. And I know I do completely mad things from time to time, and I'm sure it's because part of me just doesn't care all that much. You know - why should anyone care about anything when someone in a position of such responsibility can take everything away from you in a moment? You can't trust anyone if you can't trust a doctor."

"I understand. Thank you for telling me all this."

I sit quietly and look out of the sitting room window, there's a gust of wind which lifts the rose petals lift into the air. I watch them as they drift away, into the Autumn skies. The rose petals that Ted put there for me. My lovely Ted. I'm glad I told him. I have a feeling that the future with him is going to be pretty awesome.

"We can go to the bedroom now, if you want," I say. "Just to lie down and cuddle and chat."

He looks at me with eyes full of love.

I'm so lucky to have found him and I know we're going to have a wonderful time together. Hopefully a lovely life together.

And it's Christmas soon. Christmas! My absolutely favourite time of the year. I have a feeling it's going to be a rather adventurous and fun one…

F ancy reading about Mary Brown's antics at Christmas? Want to find out how our heroine finds herself being invited to decorate the Beckhams' Christmas tree, dressing up as Father Christmas, declaring live on This Morning that she's a drug addict and enjoying two Christmas lunches in quick succession? Just click here to continue the tale:

CLICK HERE:

UK: My Book

US: My Book

14. LOTS MORE BOOKS TO ENJOY

$\mathcal{M}$ORE BOOKS TO ENJOY

BOOK ONE:
Diary of an Adorable Fat Girl
Mary Brown is funny, gorgeous and bonkers. She's also about six stone overweight. When she realises she can't cross her legs, has trouble bending over to tie her shoelaces without wheezing like an elderly chain-smoker, and discovers that even her hands and feet look fat, it's time to take action. But what action? She's tried every diet under the sun. This is the story of what happens when Mary joins 'Fat Club' where she meets a cast of funny characters and one particular man who catches her eye.
CLICK HERE:
My Book

. . .

BOOK TWO:
Adventures of an Adorable Fat Girl

Mary can't get into any of the dresses in Zara (she tries and fails. It's messy!). Still, what does she care? She's got a lovely new boyfriend whose thighs are bigger than hers (yes!!!) and all is looking well…except when she accidentally gets herself into several thousand pounds worth of trouble at a silent auction, has to eat her lunch under the table in the pub because Ted's workmates have spotted them, and suffers the indignity of having a young man's testicles dangled into her face on a party boat to Amsterdam. Oh, and then there are all the issues with the hash-cakes and the sex museum. Besides all those things – everything's fine…just fine!

CLICK HERE:

My Book

BOOK THREE:
Crazy Life of an Adorable Fat Girl

The second course of 'Fat Club' starts and Mary reunites with the cast of funny characters who graced the first book. But this time there's a new Fat Club member…a glamorous blonde who Mary takes against. We also see Mary facing troubles in her relationship with the wonderful Ted, and we discover why she has been suffering from an eating disorder for most of her life. What traumatic incident in Mary's past has caused her all these problems?

The story is tender and warm, but also laugh-out-loud funny. It will resonate with anyone who has dieted, tried to keep up with any sort of exercise programme or spent 10 minutes in a changing room trying to extricate herself from a way-too-small garment that she ambitiously tried on and became completely stuck in.

CLICK HERE:

My Book

. . .

BOOK FOUR:
The first three books combined
This is the first three Fat Girl books altogether in one fantastic, funny package
CLICK HERE:
My Book

BOOK FIVE:
Christmas with Adorable Fat Girl
It's the Adorable Fat Girl's favourite time of year and she embraces it with the sort of thrill and excitement normally reserved for toddlers seeing Jelly Tots. Our funny, gorgeous and bonkers heroine finds herself dancing from party to party, covered in tinsel, decorating the Beckhams' Christmas tree, dressing up as Father Christmas, declaring live on *This Morning* that she's a drug addict, and enjoying two Christmas lunches in quick succession. She's the party queen as she stumbles wildly from disaster to disaster. A funny little treasure to see you smiling through the festive period.
CLICK HERE:
My Book

BOOK SIX:
Adorable Fat Girl Shares her Weight-Loss Tips
As well as having a crazy amount of fun at Fat Club, Mary also loses weight: a massive 40 lbs!! How does she do it? Here in this mini book – for the first time – she describes the rules that helped her. Also included are the stories of readers who have written in to share their weight-loss stories. This is a kind approach to weight loss. It's about learning to love yourself as you shift the pounds. It worked for Mary Brown and everyone at Fat Club (even Ted who can't go a day without a bag of chips and thinks a pint isn't a pint without a bag of pork scratchings). I hope it works for you, and I hope you enjoy it.

CLICK HERE: My Book

BOOK SEVEN:
Adorable Fat Girl on Safari

Mary Brown, our fabulous, full-figured heroine, is off on safari with an old school friend. What could possibly go wrong? Lots of things, it turns out. Mary starts off on the wrong foot by turning up dressed in a ribbon-bedecked bonnet, having channelled Meryl Streep in *Out of Africa*. She falls in lust with a khaki-clad ranger half her age and ends up stuck in a tree wearing nothing but her knickers, while sandwiched between two inquisitive baboons. It's never dull.

CLICK HERE:
My Book

BOOK EIGHT:
Cruise with an Adorable Fat Girl

Mary is off on a cruise. It's the trip of a lifetime... featuring eat-all-you-can buffets and a trek through Europe with a 96-year-old widower called Frank and a flamboyant Spanish dancer called Juan Pedro. Then there's the desperately handsome captain, the appearance of an ex-boyfriend on the ship, the time she's mistaken for a Hollywood film star in Lisbon, and tons of clothes shopping all over Europe.

CLICK HERE:
My Book

BOOK NINE:
Adorable Fat Girl Takes up Yoga

The Adorable Fat Girl needs to do something to get fit. What about yoga? I mean – really – how hard can that be? A bit of chanting, some toe touching and a new leotard. Easy! She signs up for a weekend retreat, packs up assorted snacks and heads for the countryside to get in touch with her chi and her third eye. And that's when it all goes wrong. Featuring frantic chickens, an unexpected mud bath, men in loose-fitting shorts and no pants, calamitous headstands, a new bizarre friendship with a yoga guru, and a quick hospital trip.

CLICK HERE:

My Book

BOOK TEN:
The first three holiday books combined

This is a combination book containing three of the books in my holiday series: Adorable Fat Girl on Safari, Cruise with an Adorable Fat Girl and Adorable Fat Girl takes up Yoga.

CLICK HERE:

My Book

BOOK ELEVEN:
Adorable Fat Girl and the Mysterious Invitation

Mary Brown receives an invitation to a funeral. The only problem is: she has absolutely no idea who the guy who's died is. She's told that the deceased invited her on his deathbed, and he's very keen for her to attend, so she heads off to a dilapidated old farm house in a remote part of Wales. When she gets there, she discovers that only five other people have been invited to the funeral. None of them knows who he is either. NO ONE GOING TO THIS FUNERAL HAS EVER HEARD OF THE DECEASED. Then they are told they have 20 hours to work out why they have been invited, in order to inherit a million pounds.

Who is this guy and why are they there? And what of the ghostly goings on in the ancient old building?

CLICK HERE:

My Book

. . .

BOOK TWELVE
Adorable Fat Girl goes to Weight-Loss Camp
Mary Brown heads to Portugal for a weight-loss camp
and discovers it's nothing like she expected. "I thought it would be
Slimming World in the sunshine, but this is bloody torture," she says,
after boxing, running, sand training (sand training?), more running,
more star jumps and eating nothing but carrots. Mary wants to hide
from the instructors and cheat the system. The trouble is, her mum is
with her, and won't leave her alone for a second. Then there's the
angry instructor with the deep, dark secret about why he left the
army; and the mysterious woman who sneaks into their pool and does
synchronised swimming every night. Who the hell is she? Why's she
in their pool? And what about Yvonne – the slim, attractive lady who
disappears every night after dinner. Where's she going? And what
unearthly difficulties will Mary get herself into when she decides to
follow her to find out?
CLICK HERE:
My Book

BOOK THIRTEEN:
The first two weight-loss books:
This is Weight-Loss Tips and Weight-Loss Camp
together.
CLICK HERE:
My Book

BOOK FOURTEEN:
Adorable Fat Girl goes Online Dating
She's big, beautiful and bonkers, and now she's going
online dating. Buckle up and prepare for trouble, laughter and total
chaos. Mary Brown is gorgeous, curvaceous and wants to find a

boyfriend. But where's she going to meet someone new? She doesn't want to hang around pubs all evening (actually that bit's not true), and she doesn't want to have to get out of her pyjamas unless really necessary (that bit's true). There's only one thing for it – she will launch herself majestically onto the dating scene. Aided and abetted by her friends, including Juan Pedro and best friend Charlie, Mary heads out on NINE DATES IN NINE DAYS.

She meets an interesting collection of men, including those she nicknames: Usain Bolt, Harry the Hoarder, and Dead Wife Darren. Then just when she thinks things can't get any worse, Juan organises a huge, entirely inadvisable party at the end. It's internet dating like you've never known it before.

CLICK HERE:

My Book

B OOK FIFTEEN: Adorable Fat Girl and the Six-Week Transformation

Can Mary Brown lose weight, smarten up and look fabulous enough to win back the love of her life? And can she do it in just six weeks?

In this romantic comedy from the award-winning, best-selling, Adorable Fat Girl series, our luscious heroine goes all out to try and win back the affections of Ted, her lovely ex-boyfriend. She becomes convinced that the way to do it is by putting herself through a six-week transformation plan in time for her friend's 30th birthday party that Ted is coming to. But, like most things in Mary Brown's life, things don't go exactly according to plan.

Featuring drunk winter Olympics, an amorous fitness instructor, a crazy psychic, spying, dieting, exercising and a trip to hospital with a Polish man called Lech.

CLICK HERE:

My Book

. . .

BOOK SIXTEEN: Adorable Fat Girl and the Reunion
The book opens at an exciting time. Our gorgeous, generously proportioned heroine is about to be reunited with Ted – her lovely, kind, thoughtful, wonderful ex-boyfriend. She is still madly in love with him, but how does he feel about her? Will love blossom once more? Or has Ted moved on and met someone else?

Featuring river boats, a wild psychic, a lost dog, a gallant rescue operation by a glamorous Spanish dancer named Juan, lots of gossip, fun, silliness and a huge, glorious love story…but is the love story about Ted and Mary or someone else entirely?

CLICK HERE:

My Book

SUNSHINE COTTAGE BOOKS
Also read Bernice's romantic fiction in the Sunshine Cottage series about the Lopez girls, based in gorgeous Cove Bay, Carolina.

CLICK HERE:

My Book

THE WAGS BOOKS
Meet Tracie Martin, the crazy Wag with a mission to change the world… CLICK BELOW:

Wag's Diary
My Book

. . .

Wags in LA
      My Book

Wags at the World Cup
      My Book

Printed in Great Britain
by Amazon